BLUE FRUIT

Adam Lively was born in Swansea in 1961 and studied history and philosophy in England and America. He has published two novels *Blue Fruit* (1988) and *The Burnt House* (1989), a novella *The Snail* (1991), and a pamphlet in Chatto Counterblasts series, *Parliament: The Great British Democracy Swindle* (1990). His work has also appeared in the anthologies *20 Under 35*, *P.E.N. New Poetry II* and *The Dylan Companion*.

Selected as one of The Best of Young British Novelists in 1993, his new novel *Sing the Body Electric*, is published by Chatto & Windus.

He lives in London with his wife, Diana, and their son Jacob

Adam Lively

BLUE FRUIT

V

VINTAGE

VINTAGE
20 Vauxhall Bridge Road, London SW1V 2SA

London Melbourne Sydney Auckland Johannesburg
and agencies throughout the world

First published in Great Britain by
Simon & Schuster Ltd, 1988
Sceptre edition 1989
Vintage edition 1993

2 4 6 8 10 9 7 5 3 1

Printed and bound in Great Britain by
Cox & Wyman, Reading, Berkshire

ISBN 0 09 932151 3

TO GREG

BLUE FRUIT

Dear Father,

I shall never see you again. As a gesture of farewell, I am sending you this account of all that I have seen and done since leaving Japan. I hope you will not take it ill. For to represent one's experiences by writing them down is to defy and steal from Time; and you, I think, are much in awe of that god. When I picture you now you are at your nightly ritual of winding the family clock. You fuss over the mechanism like a priest over his sacrament. You are making a prayer and an obeisance. Well I have attempted to escape that thraldom. But the family gods return to haunt one, and if I am to be truly free I must grapple a last time with that potent demon.

One afternoon, three months into this present year of 1787, I was walking by the harbour at Shimizu when my attention was caught by a young man of my own age. I don't know what it was that attracted me – perhaps it was the fact that he spoke Russian, which I had learnt as a child from Monsieur Yepanchin. Anyway, I sat down to observe him. He was supervising the unloading of a whaling vessel that had docked that morning, barking orders to a group of sailors who were heaving huge barrels from the bowels of the ship and stacking them on the quay. At one point a sailor lost his footing and dropped his end of the barrel. It crashed to the ground with a horrible splintering sound, and the precious oil began to spill out over the stone paving. The young man in charge cried out in English, 'Christ damn you, man!' and leapt down from his perch to turn the barrel the other way up, thus preventing yet more oil from escaping. Having salvaged the situation, and after yelling something in Russian at the culprit, he returned to his seat.

I was intrigued; it was many months since I had heard English spoken. So I waited. It was some hours before the operation was completed, and when it was done the sailors dispersed and the young man leant back and closed his eyes against the rays of the setting sun. I went across to him and introduced myself.

'Ah,' he said, 'an Englishman. I noticed you watching us.' He spoke English with a strong accent, as though his tongue were thick and heavy in his mouth.

'I heard you speak my language.'

He laughed and leant forward. 'I always curse in English. You have such good curses.'

His name was Sergei, and he was captain of the whaler. His father owned a fleet of ships, including the one before us. He had just returned from an expedition south through the Indies. When the ship was refitted and spring advanced a bit, he would be setting out again, but this time in a north-easterly direction. Summer, he told me, was the time to catch whales in the vast waters south of the Aleutian Islands. It was getting cold by the harbour. Sergei asked me whether I would care to dine with him, and we walked together up into the town.

We were soon close friends. He confided details of his past to me, and I to him. We shared dreams of the future. In a strange way he reminded me of Monsieur Yepanchin, my violin teacher, and the only other Russian with whom I have formed a close acquaintance. Like Sergei, Yepanchin had an expansiveness, yet in his case it was contained in the smallest of musical gestures, the slightest of movements by his long, bony fingers on the strings of his violin. The awful vicissitudes of his family – his brother, a diplomat, had fallen out of favour at the Russian court, and they were all forced to flee the country – scarcely seemed to have touched him, apart from a tendency toward irritability. He was a man lit up solely by musical phenomena, a man for whom a single note could contain whole worlds. I found in him, and in Sergei, not the darkness of spirit we associate with a frozen land, but a fervour, a hothouse of dreams and inventions. They were both the kind of people who reach outward with magnificent gestures, and become irksome and dry when they turn inward and describe themselves – the kind of people who make the worst of conversationalists, and the finest of whalers or musicians.

Over the ensuing weeks, Sergei and I met every evening. I explained to him my situation: how I had been a physician on a slave ship; how I had deserted the slave trade in order to travel to the East; how I had spent the last two years travelling through the Indies on various boats; and how I now found myself stranded in Shimizu without a position on a ship. It became established that I would join his ship as surgeon for the forthcoming expedition. The arrangement was as casual and natural as could be.

Sergei grew more and more impatient to be off. But our departure was delayed by a series of violent storms that swept in off the ocean. Two or three times we were all set to go, when the winds would begin to rattle the riggings in the harbour, the rain would lash down, and we would be obliged to bide our time. At last, when the weather seemed to be set fair, we put out to sea. For a few days all went well. Then we were buffeted by squalls. These grew larger, became storms, and for a month we battled on through perilous seas. Sergei was impatient and eager. He often ran the ship ahead of the most ferocious winds, under full sail. There were constant arguments with Borkin, the ship's mate, who favoured a more cautious approach. Sergei's enthusiasm fascinated me, and since the crew were both robustly healthy and mistrustful of me, I had plenty of leisure to observe him. His eye seemed fixed permanently on a distant goal, which gave him latitude for an engaging humour and stoicism in coping with the dangers that lay along our way. These seemed to increase with every day that passed, until, when we were almost two months out of Shimizu, we were struck by the most violent storm of all. For a week we were hurled about by waves the size of mountains, driven in circles without any idea of what course we were following, and forced to retreat below deck, there to pray each to our private gods for deliverance.

And then as suddenly as it had come, the storm ceased. We were becalmed. A dense mist closed in around us, and we drifted through it on the currents. Things passed thus for ten days, then the mist began to lift a little and we sighted land. It was low-lying, a thin wedge that forced itself into the horizon between sea and sky. We followed the coast south on the winds that had whipped up after the calm and dispersed all but the faintest wisps of mist. For a week we sailed south, and the coast never changed. I was on deck all the daylight hours, watching the coast pass slowly by. Sergei kept us at least a mile off shore to avoid sandbanks.

The land seemed to heave itself out of the sea with an enormous effort. Behind that narrow frontage, it seemed, there was a continental vastness, and something both monotonous and compelling in the experience of watching it drift by infected the crew with a strange listlessness. Draped around the decks, they scrutinised sullenly the unfolding panorama of sand and rock. For my own part, a great excitement was beginning to stir. Out of the chaos of the past weeks, when everything had been dictated by the destructiveness of the sea, there was crystallising within me a curiosity, a mad and wayward desire to explore this land.

I communicated my interest to Sergei, but his mind was on the practicalities of whaling. In a couple of days, he told me, he would send a party ashore, but only to collect some fresh water. Then they would be heading straight out to sea again. I urged him further.

'Only a week,' I said. 'We could spare a week to explore inland. Who knows what we would find! I know the whaling must come first, but the crew could do with some rest ashore, and a week would make so little difference. We have no idea what might be there, what we could miss.'

Something in the way he shook his head, and his condescending smile, infuriated me. I was on the point of remonstrating with him some more, when there was a shout from the crow's nest. We looked up. The lookout was pointing off to starboard, and somewhat astern. We scrambled across the deck and looked out to sea. The setting sun's rays slanted across the water, and for a moment I was dazzled. But then I could see them. Three orcas were racing through the water some four hundred yards away. They swam almost parallel to the ship, though even as we watched they veered slightly out to sea.

I had seen orcas once before off Madagascar. But that had been under a tropical sun, with the heat sticky between my legs. How different it was now to stand looking out below a sky washed of all but the palest blue, on a sea chopped into wavelets by the wind, in this slightly chill northern spring. But the orcas were the same, the same flash of the white flank before the animal dipped again below the surface of the sea. The deck rang with excited talk as the men watched the animals.

'It was two years ago last autumn, I tell you,' a sailor beside me was saying to his companion. 'They came at night, a dozen of them, and milled around the ship for hours. Wouldn't leave us alone, even bumping the hull they were. Anyway, at dawn they sets off out of the bay where we was anchored and then wheels around and comes back to the ship and does that performance of swimming around the ship again. So they do this a couple of times and then our skipper gets the message and ups anchor and follows them. Once we're doing that, they drops the palaver of milling round the ship, and leads us all morning up the coast to this other bay where there's the juiciest bunch of Bottlenose whales you've ever seen. We had a massacre that day, let me tell you. And them orcas were right there in the thick of it, getting all the pickings. One calf we harpooned we didn't even bring in. The orcas got to it first and by the time they'd had a taste there wasn't enough of the damn thing left to make it worth our while. Yup, those orcas had the whole thing worked out from the beginning. And when they'd done with gobbling up the offal that we chucked over they does a couple of circuits round the ship before they go like they're saying "It's been nice doing business with you, gentlemen!" Ha ha ha.'

At sunset the mist closed in again and filled the space between the ship and the coast. As the light faded the land had become a menacing strip of indeterminate colour. I had been brooding. In my mind I had already left the ship, and was exploring the land that lay before me like a token of promise and threat. Sergei's enthusiasm over the incident of the orcas had fired my own, divergent ambition. I was twenty-four years old. My life was an unrealised void. I could not return on the paths by which I had come: I must needs press on down the path I had fashioned for myself. My mind was made up. With a shiver, I stood up and stretched my legs, which were stiff from sitting on the cold deck, crossed the foredeck, and entered Sergei's cabin without knocking.

He was stooped over a chart that was spread out on the table before him. He heard me enter, but did not look up.

'They were heading south-west,' he said.

'So you believe those stories too, about orcas leading ships to whales?'

'In a sense.' His full lips, red from the evening air, were drawn sideways in a smile. Orcas, he explained, are scavengers, often to be found following large whale herds in order to pick off the young and the sick. Although an orca would rarely attack a healthy adult sperm whale, it could well make a meal of a member of the herd that had fallen behind the others and was less able to defend itself. Stories of orcas deliberately leading whalers to a herd of whales could, he admitted, be fanciful. But it was easy to see how they had arisen: follow orcas and you will often come to whales.

He gave the explanation in an energetic and engaging manner, but something within me rebelled. I listened in polite silence. When he had finished, I said, 'Sergei, I've been thinking further about exploring this land we've come across. My heart's set on it. If, as you say, there is no question of a party from the ship going ashore for any length of time, then I must ask you to relieve me of my duties and allow me to take this course alone. I must own that I would not be a great loss to the ship. The crew ignore me, and I can provide them with no assistance without their cooperation. Indeed, I think they despise me, for being a foreigner, and for having secured a position on the ship, as they see it, solely through my friendship with you.'

For a moment he looked at me in amazement. Then, frowning, he looked down again at the chart on the table. 'Of course, you're a free man,' he said, 'and must do as you please. At dawn we'll lower a boat. They can drop you and look around for water at the same time. And then we're going to get onto the trail of those orcas. Did you see the way they were moving? They had a purpose, John. I'll swear they're following a herd. If we keep hard after them, they'll lead us to sperms. I'm sure of it.'

He was hurt, I could tell. But there was nothing I could say to make it any better. He inquired solicitously whether I would be able to survive alone in a foreign land, and I assured him. We talked on into the night while the flame of the candle complained in its pool of wax. It was as though the longer we huddled together over the chart – he to project the possible course of the orcas, I to estimate where on the coast I might land the following day – the more we curled in on ourselves and the more our surroundings receded. There was something obsessive and introverted that acted as a gravitational force drawing us together. Each of us followed his private speculation and the polite interest each of us took in the other's project might have appeared to an observer somewhat forced. But all the more, I think I can say when I look back on our close and distant friendship, that that interest was an achievement, a gesture of curious love. We were as two planets that passed through vast space and – somehow, miraculously – acknowledged each other.

This could equally well be Sergei's tale, Father. Think of two shoots from a single branch. As one grows more successfully, reaches the sunlight where its leaves can spread and its flowers blossom, it attracts the vital forces from the common root. The sap rises into it and deprives the other, which withers and dies. Sergei and I, deep down, were so alike that it seemed to me we tapped the same force in just that way; my flourishing depended on his decay.

But this is my story, and I shall confine it to myself. I left Sergei and retired to bed. As I lay in the darkness, I was afflicted by the most violent turmoil of the brain. They were not thoughts that raced through my skull, nor even images, but a kind of pure energy. It seemed to rush from a source deep in my neck and crash forward in a great arc through my forehead. And it had a texture that was somehow both soft and amorphous, and as sharp and dangerous as a razor. The sensation was frightening and fascinating. The velocity of this energy increased as I kept my eyes shut, till I could take it no more, and opened my eyes to gaze around my cabin, which was dappled with the moonlight that filtered down through the hatch. The sensation subsided but did not cease. When I closed my eyes it started up again with mounting force. This sequence repeated itself several times. My body remained outwardly still and calm. Eventually I drifted off to sleep.

*　　　*　　　*

A ship at sea, an enclosed and claustrophobic community, is
given to violent collective gusts of emotion. When I rose at
dawn the next day the mist still hung heavily in the air, but
among the crew the lethargy of the past days was dispelled,
replaced by a tense activity. By the time I had packed my
belongings (a spare trouser, a shirt, my knife, spare laces, and
a leather jerkin) into a canvas sack and mounted the steps
onto the deck, the men had been up and about for some time.
Above me, two men who had been sent up the main mast to
adjust some rigging swapped banter and instructions. The
moisture that was thick in the air between the masts and sails
seemed to amplify the thick rolling sounds of their Russian. At
the stern, the men who would make up the landing party were
struggling to unload from the boat the sails that had been
stored there. One of them was smaller and weaker than the
others, and when he periodically dropped his end of the heavy
rolls of canvas he was roundly cursed by the others in the
group. The mist was thick with the tangy rotting smell of
seaweed that fills the air where sea meets land.

I walked down the ship and began to converse with Borkin,
the mate, who was supervising the men. We talked of the
weather; he was confident the wind would freshen and disperse
the mist. Borkin – a man of level-headed vapidity – was the only
one of the Russians apart from Sergei with whom I had reasonably
cordial relations. I had tried for a while to make some contact
with the men, but it always ended in my retreating in seething
embarrassment. Their conversation revolved around two things
– carnality and endless, tedious leg-pulling and name-calling.
When I joined one of their groups as they sat around in the
evenings or during a calm, they were inclined to ignore me for
long stretches, then one of them would utter to me some absurd
inanity or gibberish. Welcoming a chance to enter in with them,
I would ask him to make himself clearer, and the whole group
would roar with laughter and mock me for my stupidity. The
injustice of this, from such yahooish fools, would keep me awake
at night. And then I would curse myself for paying such note to
them, until, what with cursing myself and the injustice by turn, I
would be in the blackest humour.

Even as Borkin and I talked, one of those man-handling the sails made a noise like breaking wind, and when we looked round, the whole group was grinning up at me. I turned on my heel, and as I retreated along the deck I heard Borkin telling them firmly to return to their work.

Sergei was standing alone on the foredeck looking out to sea from the starboard bow, as though he were still watching the orcas speeding out through the grey waters. I joined him. The sun by now had evaporated the upper layers of mist, and the swathe of moisture that remained low around the ship and across the sea was rapidly disappearing as the sun penetrated the atmosphere with ever greater intensity. It would be a warm day. Sergei was not to join the landing party, and we had just begun an awkward farewell, when Borkin shouted down the ship to Sergei that the boat had been lowered. We walked down the length of the ship, I picked up my sack where I had left it, and clambered down into the boat. That was the last time I ever saw Sergei.

It took an hour to reach the shore. Once we were away from the ship, the sky, which was now clear of all but the faintest wisps of mist, seemed to open like a flower. I was suddenly aware of how my perception those past weeks had been circumscribed by the ship, by the ever-present masts and messy tangles of rigging that partitioned the sky every time one looked up. Now a great void opened above me. There were eight of us in the party – the six oarsmen, Borkin, and myself – along with ten large barrels that had been squeezed in between the men. Borkin sat in the stern, directing the oarsmen, while I sat in the bows, where normally the harpooneer would be stationed to lean out over the foaming water.

Watching the broad backs of the oarsmen strain against the oars, I was uncomfortably aware of my status as a passenger – of less use than the dead weight of the barrels that kept the boat low in the water – and of the gulf between myself and the Russians that I had never bridged. I clutched my sack closer to my chest and twisted around awkwardly to view the shore as we approached it. Our course was bringing us to the southern end of a broad bay. The land rose no more than fifty feet high behind the beach, and was dotted with what looked like bushes or small trees. It was utterly still.

And this was all there seemed to be. To north and south the beaches stretched away just the same. Even some quarter of a mile off shore the water was only to the depth of a man's chest. The men, who had kept up an endless stream of breathy talk out in open water, fell silent. Two hundred yards from shore we jumped from the boat and pulled it in.

I think I had imagined that I had but to mount that slope behind the beach, and the whole of the country would be spread before me – the fields, the villages, the meadows. It was not to be like that. Once out of the water, I dashed up the sand to the crest of the hill, but all I could see from there was a shallow gully and another gentle hill. I returned to the men, who were unloading the barrels. It felt odd to have solid ground beneath my feet. The yellow of the sand and the green of the thin grass that grew in clumps on the dunes dazzled me.

Borkin directed three of the men to stay with the boat and the barrels while the others accompanied him to search for water. I tagged along with them.

We set off south along the ridge behind the beach. To our left lay the sand dunes, with their desolate bushes, and to our right the beaches that curved in and out, forming wide bays. We had gone about two miles when, happening to look back down the coast, I saw someone running along the beach in our direction. I drew Borkin's attention to this and the whole group crouched down and watched. Though she was still some way off, we could see that it was a woman. I would say a lady, but never before had I seen a lady dressed and behaving in such a manner. She was wearing the shortest of men's short trousers and a loose fitting vest that flapped about her chest. Her hair was long and fair, and tied into a kind of bunch at the back, so that it flowed behind her like the tail of a horse at full gallop. Her cheeks puffed with effort, and the expression on her face was serious and intent.

I was mystified. It could not have been that we had startled her and made her flee, for she was approaching us and had given no indication that she was aware of our presence on the ridge above. Perhaps she was escaping the men who were guarding the boat further down the coast – yet there was no sign of them.

Through a whispered discussion with Borkin it was decided that as she drew parallel with our position I should hail her in English and impress upon her the friendliness of our intentions. She might well be able to tell us where we could find water. She pounded along the sand towards us, her hair flipping jauntily from side to side. My moment arrived. I stood up and called out, 'Madam! We are foreign sailors. We mean you no harm.'

Her reaction was most deflating. Without faltering in her stride she looked up, smiled, and waved her hand at us.

A dumbfounded silence fell on our group as we watched her pass us and race away up the beach. I looked down at the other men and shrugged my shoulders. They stood up from their crouching positions.

'Come on then, let's get after her,' said one of them.

There was a growl of assent from his companions. At this point I stepped in: knowing the men, and in view of their long separation from that sex, I had doubts as to their motives. I quickly protested to Borkin that we had no time to go chasing along beaches, for we had to get on with looking for water. He thought for a moment, his stolid face immobile, and then agreed with me. He ordered them to hold back. I felt a shudder of resentment run through the group of men. They glowered at me.

A half a mile further along the coast we came across a small stream that cut a shallow gully through the ridge and flowed on out onto the beach. Borkin reckoned it was sufficient for their purpose, and instructed everybody to return to the boat for the barrels, which they would then fill and roll back along the beach. I decided to leave them at this point, and told them as much. The farewell was not a fond one – merely a deferential nod from Borkin before the whole lot of them turned and marched away from me.

I was now alone, and the sight of the waves sliding up over the sand cast me into a melancholy frame. I longed to turn from the coast and head straight inland to search for civilisation. Yet reason told me to continue up along the coast till I should find, say, a river to follow. Better that than wandering without direction. The sun rose higher and the day warmed. The land grew more hilly, and the ridge upon which I walked became a cliff rising some two hundred feet above the beach. I was walking now through the long grass, and the effort of it tired me. At about midday I lay down to rest, and fell into a light sleep. At one point I woke briefly. Or perhaps it was a dream. At any rate, I sat up and looked out at the sea. From up on the cliff, its vastness was overwhelming. The sun glittered on it. And far, far out, just below the horizon, I thought I could see the sails of a ship retreating into that vastness.

When I awoke fully, I was disturbed to see that it was well past noon. I had that feeling of loss one experiences after sleeping during the day. Disorientated, I stood up and looked around. I could see no break in the coastline ahead, and the terrain inland seemed easy. So I made my decision and set off away from the coast. Something in the aspect of the landscape increased gradually that sense of unease to which I had awoken. Once past the sand dunes, there began an area of sparse woodland. The trees were stunted and well spaced, but provided just enough shade that the grass was short and poor. The barrenness of the place was such as one might expect to find on a high plateau; the discrepancy between this and the fact that it was no more than a couple of hundred feet above sea level gave rise, I think, to the eerie sensations I felt. It was strange for an Englishman, accustomed to the precise ordering of the countryside for the generation of plant and animal, to encounter a place of such dissipated infecundity.

But the walking was easy, and as the afternoon progressed I covered a good few miles. The slight chill in the air that heralded dusk invigorated me, and I quickened my step. With the fading light, the woods were thrown into focus by the shadows and acquired a depth and clarity they had not had during the day. For the first time since leaving the landing party I felt a sense of adventure.

As if in response to my feelings, I saw an alteration in the landscape up ahead. The trees appeared to thicken in a long line, and beyond this line there was a gap. I hurried on and scrambled through the undergrowth. I found myself in a clearing some fifteen yards across that had been cut through the wood. It stretched away in both directions as far as the eye could see. Running down the middle of it, some three feet apart and laid on cross-timbers, were two iron rails. I remember you describing something similar you had seen at a coal mine in Derbyshire. From the way the clearing cut diagonally across the route I had taken from the sea, I guessed it had come from the coast way up towards the north. I turned and began to follow the rails in the other direction – southward and inland.

My boots crunched on the stones of the track. As darkness closed, a blanket of low cloud was drawn over the land. This would keep in some of the day's warmth; I was glad. The trees on either side thinned, and I came out into open, flat country. I could tell it was flat by the lights shining far away on either horizon. Up ahead in the distance was a mysterious pale glow, tinged with orange. I did not feel in the least tired, and was happy to walk on through the darkness. By the strange paleness on the horizon ahead, and by the weak moonlight that seeped through from time to time when the clouds thinned, I was able to see that the track had widened and other sets of rails had joined the one I was following. The lights sprinkled in the distance varied in brightness. They were yellow and orange. Some of them blinked on and off.

Fatigue began to ache in my head and feet. I had wandered to the edge of the track, and just ahead of me I could make out a dark shape, a building just off the track. It was a wooden hut. I edged carefully around it and discovered first a window that had been smashed in, and then a door that gave easily to my shoulder. Once inside, weariness overcame me quickly. Without even inspecting my surroundings, I curled up on the floor and put my sack under my head.

The next moment it was daylight and I was looking up at the cobweb on the sloping ceiling of the hut. There were voices outside. I scrambled to my feet and moved to the door. As I put my hand to the handle, the door was pushed firmly open from the outside. Facing me was a big man with a round face topped by a blue peaked cap, wearing baggy blue leggings that reached right

up over his shoulders. For a couple of seconds he looked at me
blankly, then he turned his head and shouted, 'Hey! We got
ourselves a bum in the shed here.'

He looked back at me. 'You been sleeping here?'

'Yes. I was . . .'

'Whassat?' The man's companion appeared from around the
corner of the hut.

He was dressed identically to the other, but was an African.
When he saw me he stopped.

''S he been sleeping in there?'

'Says so.'

'Godammit.' The African shook his head, as though more
grieved than angry.

The big man's eyes had alighted on the door.

'You do that?' He indicated with a nod of his head where the
wood had splintered away from the frame during my breaking in.

'I'm afraid so. Please understand I was tired from walking from
the coast. You see the ship I was on . . .'

'You're way outta line doing that, mister. Hell, we could bring
charges. Come on, let's see what else he's done in here.'

He advanced through the doorway, followed by the African; I
retreated before them. Once inside, the two men seemed self-
consciously to relax. The big man slumped into a chair, took off
his cap, ran his hand over his bald pate as though smoothing down
imaginary hair, and replaced the cap deftly by fitting it at the back
and then jamming it down over his eyes. The African placed the
lantern he was carrying on the workbench that ran the length of
the hut, then set about lighting the stove.

Above the workbench was the window I had discovered the
previous night. The glass that was intact was so dirty that nothing
was visible through it but the vaguest impression of brown and
grey, surmounted by the blue of the sky. Through that part of
the window which was smashed came a blast of chill early morning
air. I shifted slightly so that I could see out. There were the rails,
about six sets of them, and beyond that some dilapidated buildings.
The blue sky, rich with the promise of the heat to come later in
the day, was criss-crossed by wires and lines strung from poles
above the rails. It reminded me of the rigging on the ship.

The two men seemed to have forgotten about me. The African was filling a small pot with water from a kind of pump in the corner, while his companion looked slowly about the room. I was on the point of speaking up, to set things straight and start them off afresh, when the big man said, 'Well, you don't seem to have done any damage. We'll let it pass this time.'

'Gentlemen,' I began. My moment had come.

I then recounted my story: how I was from England; how my ship, a Russian whaler, had got lost in storms and fetched up off the coast; how I had determined to leave the ship and explore the country; how we had seen the orcas and how Sergei had set himself to pursuing them; how I had landed with the party assigned to look for water; how we had encountered the woman running on the beach; and how, having left them, I had discovered the rails and followed them during the night to this place.

There was a long silence. The big man was cleaning the dirt from under his fingernails with a sliver of wood. The African was behind me at the stove; I could just hear him quietly moving things about. Then the big man leaned forward and began untying and retying the laces of his boots.

'Well, now that you're here,' he said at the floor, 'I hope you'll have a profitable stay. You sure won't find a better place on earth.'

There was another awkward pause. I sensed almost a feeling of disapproval in the air. I looked round at the African. He started when our eyes met and busied himself again at the stove, saying 'I guess you'll be hungry.'

'Yeah,' broke in the big man. 'Give the man some coffee and a bite to eat.'

So I ate and drank with them. It was a difficult meal: they were most polite, but showed no inclination to ask me questions. This inhibited me, and though there were many things I wished to ask about their country, I stayed quiet.

Swigging off the last of his coffee, the big man stood up, nodded to the African and said to me, 'If you'll take my advice, sir, you'll sleep somewheres else but railway sheds.' With that he left.

Alone with the African I felt more at ease. The sun was now high above the buildings the other side of the track, and its light streamed through the broken window onto the dusty surface of the workbench. The African offered me tobacco, and we smoked together. Soon the hut was filled with delicious blue-grey smoke. I stretched out my legs and looked at the African more closely through the cosy haze. He was short, not much more than five foot, and slender. His skin was a fine deep bronze and his features were perfectly Negroid. His face was small but very round, and seemed perpetually pointing forward so that an air of delicate curiosity hung about his full lips.

'Is this your hut?' I asked.

'Jeez no. This belong to the company.' His face took on a mask of nervous animation when he spoke. 'I'm just an operative, but I'm working up to Junior Engineer. He's an engineer' (he indicated the door). 'We work nights together. See, that's the way to get ahead – nights. You get more responsibility, and it shows management that you have greater . . . commitment. Mind you, he' (indicating the door again) 'only does nights 'cause he can't stand his wife. Real no-hoper.'

The smoke swirled up to the slanting rafters. The hut was warm now from the stove and the sunlight on the window. Another question had been pressing on me. When he paused, I gave way to it and let it go.

'Are you a slave?'

I realised immediately that the question was based on a misunderstanding. I feared a violent reaction. Instead, the African broke into an exaggerated, theatrical laugh, glanced at me with a smile and shake of his head, then looked up to the rafters and said, as though addressing an imaginary audience, 'This is *weird shit*. I mean, this shit is *weird*!'

For a few moments he chuckled to himself, shaking his head and glancing at me. In his eyes were tears of laughter.

'Come over here,' he said. 'I want to show you something.' He went over to the window and, with an effort, forced it open. There was a sound of splintering wood, and the dust from the workbench danced upwards in the sunlight.

'There.'

I joined him at the window.

'This is the land of freedom.'

I peered out into the sunshine. Beneath the window was a pile of rubble. To left and right the rails dribbled away into the distance. Ahead, past the dilapidated buildings that stood by the rails, there was a vast open space crossed by more rails and littered with more rubble.

The African returned to his seat with the air of a man who had just made a conclusive point in an argument. I remained at the window for a while longer, to please him, and then sat down again myself. My companion seemed emboldened by this exchange. He smiled at me directly.

'I guess you're looking for somewhere to shack up,' he said. 'You should meet my brother, Tommy. He'll see you right. He hangs out with a lot of weird types. What's your name?'

'John Field.'

'Mine's Eldridge. Good to meet you.' We nodded to one another. 'C'mon then.'

He led me out of the hut onto the tracks. As we picked our way over the metal rails, he explained to me in detail the organisation of the railroad company. But I was distracted by new sights and sounds. Away to our right, the tracks merged into the indeterminate shape of the centre of a city, which formed a lumpish break in the horizon. My companion fell silent for a moment, and I could sense a barely audible but enormous hum from that direction, a throbbing that was caught and lost again on the fresh morning breeze blowing across the waste land.

'Lucky you got me to see you across this lot,' he said with pride as we stepped over the next set of rails. 'You gotta know when you can cross. These trains won't stop for no one. You'd be a dead man by yourself.'

I thanked him. But death and danger seemed far away in that clear, empty light. The dull browns and greys of the derelict buildings vibrated with colour.

'Yeah', he continued. 'The drivers got this new directive, you see. "Don't stop for no one." A bit tough, I guess, but then you can't endanger passengers for every nutcase that comes down here onto the tracks.'

He returned to the running of the railroad. His gaze was fixed firmly on the treacherous ground before him. He talked with singlemindedness, as though repeating something he had learnt by rote. Ahead of us was the last of the tracks, and beyond it a steep grassy bank, surmounted by tall brick houses. We began to climb the bank. The grass was long and thick. In among it lay twisted and corroded pieces of metal, the carcasses of machines. Flowers grew up through them. The sight was like that of a calm and long-abandoned ruin, the detritus of a long-dead civilisation.

We emerged onto a street of large terraced houses, all of them in a lamentable condition and many locked and boarded up. There were a few people abroad, all of them Africans, all of them scurrying along purposefully as though to escape the bleak scene. The house to which I was led was at the end of a quiet street. It was detached from its neighbours, and smaller. Cracks zigzagged down through the brickwork. My companion pushed open the door, from which the paint was peeling off in flakes, and we entered a dark corridor. My eyes were dazzled after the bright sunlight outside. Eldridge opened a door to our left and exclaimed, 'What the hell you done with the furniture?'

'Need some space, man. The boys are coming over to practise.'

'You better have it set right before the women come home. Anyway, I've got you another one for your collection.'

'What do you mean?'

'This guy. Joe and me found him down in the shed by the tracks. He's been sleeping in there. He's got some weird story about a shipwreck, so I says to him he can stay here till he finds somewhere . . .'

'You crazy?'

'Hey, come on in and meet my brother,' said Eldridge, ignoring him and taking me by the arm. 'This should be our best room. But Tommy and his freaky friends use it.' He ushered me in.

The man to whom Eldridge had been talking was standing in the middle of a bare room. At one end of it were stacked chairs and a table. The floor was bare. He was taller than his brother, and whereas Eldridge had fine and sensitive features, this man was big-boned and coarse. Around his neck was slung a musical instrument, a horn with an intricate mechanism of keys and valves.

'Tell Tommy what you were telling me,' said Eldridge. 'About the shipwreck and stuff.'

'Actually it wasn't wrecked,' I said. 'I landed here by choice. Something drew me here.'

'You *must* be crazy,' muttered the brother.

'Give the man a break,' said Eldridge. 'You go right ahead, John.'

'We got lost in a storm, and found ourselves on the coast. I wanted to explore inland, but Sergei, the captain, was determined to set out to sea again in pursuit of some orcas that we sighted. So when a party came ashore to look for water, I joined them and set out by myself.'

'You jumped ship?' said Eldridge eagerly.

'I suppose so. I had the captain's permission. I think he understood my motives, that I was seeking adventure.'

'Well, you won't find any adventure around here,' said Tommy. We regarded each other suspiciously. 'Still,' he continued, 'now you're here I guess you'll need some help.'

'That's what I figured,' said Eldridge conclusively. 'You want something to eat, John? I could do with a bite myself.'

He led me out of the door and down the corridor to a small kitchen. He cut some bread, placed on top of it some fatty meat and we sat down at the table to eat. We ate hungrily, in silence. After a few moments there came a honking sound from along the corridor.

'Jeez,' sighed Eldridge. 'Here we go.'

Tommy began a long slow scale.

Eldridge wiped his mouth. 'I've gotta get some sleep,' he said. 'You make yourself at home, won't you?'

He went out into the corridor, and I could hear him climbing the stairs. The scales continued: major, minor, then major again. Then there was an odd scale that was neither major nor minor, with tricky notes slipped into it. I looked down at the table, at the piece of bread with its slice of grey meat, and smiled at the oddity of my situation. Only the day before I had been aboard a whaling ship, and now here I was in some strangers' kitchen, in the middle of a city. Things seemed to have moved very quickly. The scales were gradually speeding up, till they were racing up

and down through three octaves. Intrigued, I picked up the piece
of bread and went along the corridor.

'Do you mind if I listen to you?'

Tommy turned round. 'Sure you can,' he said casually. 'Not
too exciting. I'm just warming up.'

I sat on the floor with my back to the wall and munched on the
bread. I had never seen his type of horn before, though I had
seen some like it – *chalumeau* instruments. It was made of brass,
but had a single reed and made a tender sound. He wandered up
and down the room as he played. His feet were bare. Once, he
caught my eye as I watched him and raised his eyebrows. After
a while he stopped to recover his breath.

'Eldridge's always getting at me about moving the furniture
around,' he said. 'Thing is, you gotta give the sound space to
move, free up the vibrations, you know.' He banged the wooden
boards with his bare feet, making a fleshy thump.

'I quite agree,' I said.

''Sides, the others'll be here soon, and there wouldn't be room
for them otherwise.'

He began playing again. He played no melodies, just disciplined
exercises. Sometimes as he played his gaze would be directed
into my eyes. But his gaze was uncomprehending, for all his
attention was on the sounds he made. This pleased me, as it
seemed to indicate that he was growing more comfortable with
my presence. When he stopped again, he sat down on the floor
opposite me. We looked at each other.

'What are you doing here anyway?' he said.

'I don't know yet.'

He nodded.

'Look, Mister Field,' he continued. 'I don't know anything about
you – where you're coming from, where you're going. But it
strikes me you don't really belong here. You sure this is where
you're meant to be?'

'I don't know where I'm meant to be. When I left the ship I
was aware that it was an odd course to take, that I was deviating
from what was expected of me and what I was meant to do. I
took a diferent path.'

'Which makes you a pretty crazy kind of traveller. If you're looking for something, adventure or fame and fortune and stuff, you got to be a little together about where you're gonna find it.'

'I'm an errant traveller, I suppose.'

He laughed. 'Errant traveller,' he said. 'I like that.'

'I suppose if I was really seeking something, like adventure, I would have stayed with Sergei in pursuit of the orcas.'

'Yeah, well, I never trust a person who's looking for something. The only people I know always looking for things are police and thieves.'

There was a long pause. Tommy whistled a tune, fingering the keys of his horn.

'Yeah, I could tell,' he said. 'You been looking for adventure, you wouldn't waste your time sitting around listening to me warming up. You'd be out there.' His attitude now was more friendly.

'Actually I have a particular interest. I'm a musician myself.'

'That right? What do you play?'

'The violin.'

'No kidding? Fiddle player. You any good?'

'I couldn't say.'

'Well, who you played with?'

'No one for some time. I've been at sea. When I was younger I used to play a lot.'

'When did you start?'

'When I was eight years old. My mother was accomplished at the keyboard. She bought a violin for me and engaged the services of a gentleman who acted as organist at a local church. He instructed me in the rudiments of the art – the attitude of the arms, hands, fingers; musical notation; the principles of string-stopping; the smooth action of the bow. As I grew in proficiency, I was allowed to take part in concerts by local orchestras. A couple of years later my father took me up to London to see a Russian gentleman. Then when I ran away from home when I was thirteen, I went to London and became apprenticed to a physician. I continued to take lessons with Monsieur Yepanchin, and played with various orchestras. Once I played at Westminster. But after a few years I had to return

home, because I had no money. My father found me a position
as a ship's physician. I've been at sea ever since that. I've travelled
the world.'

I stopped speaking. Tommy was rattling the keys of his horn.
I think I was boring him.

'Some day . . .' he began, but he was interrrupted by a clatter-
ing and banging outside the door. He got up. 'That'll be the
others,' he said.

Three more Africans struggled into the room.

The first carried a round-bellied guitar, the second an enormous
bass fiddle, while the third was laden with drums and cymbals.

'This is John Field,' said Tommy. 'He's gonna be shacking up
with us for a while. Plays fiddle.'

The three arrivals looked at me wearily and nodded, then began
setting up their instruments. The room was full of pluckings and
bangings. By now I was in a state of considerable anticipation to
hear what their music sounded like. Wherever I have been,
Father, I have sought out the music of that land, for nothing
fascinates me more. Indeed, if nothing else should come of this
letter, I would wish it to communicate to you something of my
impressions of, and enthusiasm for, the music I have found here.
Our writers on travel are so silent concerning the richness and
variety of the musics of the world. In Japan I have attended an
elaborate ritual where the performance of one piece lasted a full
three days, and I have heard the sad, simple songs of the slaves
lamenting their condition and longing for home. Yet at the same
time, what unity and harmony! Through all that kaleidoscope of
sound there run the indestructible principles of music – the
perfection of the fourth, fifth, and octave, and the resolution of
discord. Truly, music is the universal language. Man singing unto
man is understood.

As for the music of Tommy and his friends, it crept up on me
unawares. The bass fiddler was plucking deep notes from his
instrument. They wandered aimlessly, and I thought at first that
he was still tuning and testing his instrument. But then a pattern
emerged, a slow scale that rose from the depths, dipped, rose
again, then swooped down again to the point at which it had
started. Tommy was staring at the floor, swaying to the lop-sided

rhythm. As the cycle leapt down the octave, he slowly raised the horn to his lips and began to play.

He played a quiet, almost tentative, phrase. It was like a door being gently opened to reveal a scene of intimate confession. The tone was clear but soft. I was immediately and painfully transported to one hot night off the African coast when, lying on the open deck, I heard a song drift up through the hatch from the hold. That was the first time that I had heard a slave sing. It unsettled, even frightened me, for the song was as naked as the slave himself, and even to hear it, to listen to it in that hellish place, seemed a violation. Tommy's melody was smoother and in a way less strange, but I felt in it that same sense of something private made painfully, and triumphantly, public.

With these first, hesitant phrases, it was as though Tommy was establishing his voice, his right to be heard. Then the supplication in his voice grew more intense. He began to expand his gestures and use wider intervals. As the music reached an emotional crisis – a fear, perhaps, that the prayer would not be answered – the drummer lent his support. With his fat bulk crouched over the drums like a great black toad, clasping a pair of metal brushes in his hands, he began stroking one of the drums with a steady, circular rhythm. Even as one might whisk a particle of dust up into the air, the voice of Tommy's horn was buoyed up. It floated to a higher register, it sang higher and higher. And when it had reached its highest and most ethereal note, and held it almost past endurance, the sole remaining member of the band took up his guitar and started to strum out the latent harmonies. Tommy began to dance, as though the chords were gusts of wind blowing him about through the air. The fullness of the sound beneath him was like a cushion. He bounced and strutted on it. He finished phrases with slurred, ironical comments. The drummer snapped his brush down onto the cymbal, building a halo of golden sound. And at its centre, like a holy fool, was Tommy's laughing horn.

When I started this account, Father, I promised myself that I would include in it everything that should be included, even if this was at the expense of spoiling a smooth and seamless pattern. So while you will have gathered by now my enthusiasm for the music, I must put on record a reservation. When Tommy had finished his solo, the rhythm continued, and the bass fiddler attempted to take up the melody. He fumbled in the lower register, where the sound was indistinct; and he fumbled in the upper, where it was strained. The phrases were perfunctory – snatched from the mind, rather than flowing smoothly from the heart as Tommy's had done. The latter was looking at the floor again, swaying backwards and forwards, and nodding now and then as if in interest or approval. The only moment of the bass fiddler's contribution of which I approved was at the end of it, when he cleverly leapt back down to the beginning of the cycle as if he had never left it. At the same moment, Tommy entered again with a *ritornello*, but this time the melody was stated with blazing confidence. He flared up to a high note, then fell back to a few last embers at the bottom.

Nobody spoke. The drummer adjusted his drums, the bass fiddler tuned a string, Tommy sucked on his reed, wetting it, then launched straight into a quick, swirling introduction. The drummer picked up a pair of sticks and entered behind him with a rhythm like thunder. This new piece was spiky and leaping after the manner of a French *ouverture*. Tommy was off on a journey of lightning arpeggios and limber embellishment. In a moment of illumination I saw an affinity with the music I had so loved at home, that of Handel, Corelli, Vivaldi, and the Italian School. Yes, here was the same excitement, of rhythms wound up and sprung like traps. Tommy played a *concertino* part, while the others were the *ripieno*, punctuating his statements with off-beat chords that prodded and goaded him to dizzier invention.

Suddenly, the door was swung wide open. Eldridge stood there with an expression of nervous fury playing across his face.

'Will you guys keep it down,' he yelled into the room.

The music ground to a halt.

Tommy beat the air by his side with rage. 'Where do you get off doing that, brother? We were *playing*.'

'Yeah, and I was trying to sleep. I've been working all night and I'm beat.'

Tommy made a gesture of impatience.

'Yeah brother, *working*.'

'Well, we're working now.'

'Go "work" some place else.'

'Yeah, and you go down town and ask the mayor if he'll let us use city hall for the day.'

'Fuck you.'

'Yeah, and you have a nice day too, Eldridge.'

Eldridge slammed the door shut. There was a long silence. Tommy looked at his horn and frowned.

'Let's take a break,' he muttered. 'I'll get us some beers.'

There was much sighing and shrugging of shoulders as the others put down their instruments. Tommy returned with some bottles and passed them round.

'You reckon you could play our kind of music then, Mister Field?' he asked when we were all seated on the floor.

'Perhaps. There were things about it that were familiar.'

'Like what?'

'Well, that bass line you played in the first piece is what I would call a ground bass.'

They all laughed.

'I like that,' said Tommy.

'Yeah,' exclaimed the drummer, 'it's like you crawl along down there real close to the ground.'

'What else?' asked Tommy, who was thoroughly amused and interested by now.

I thought for a moment. 'You improvise long passages and add your own embellishments to the melody. Well, I learnt to do that. Monsieur Yepanchin . . .'

'Monsieur who?' asked Tommy, laughing.

'Yepanchin. He was my teacher. He insisted that I learn how to improvise. He always said that a musician who could not do that was just a machine.'

'Yeah,' put in the guitarist earnestly. 'You gotta know how to play the changes.'

'What else then?' asked Tommy.

'Something in the pace of the music, and the speed of its movement from one moment to the next . . .'

'You're dead right,' said Tommy. 'This is working music. If you can't hold the attention of that audience, you're lost. They ain't gonna reverently sit there while you indulge yourself. This ain't the classics. You gotta get it across.'

'Else they're gonna start throwing things at you,' added the drummer.

'Mind you,' continued Tommy, 'I like an audience like that. Shows they're listening.' He laughed. 'You don't get too many crowds like that nowadays. Some of the guys you hear around these days, the reason they're so tame is they've never had to try.'

Time drifted on. Tommy fetched some more beer. The musicians began playing again.

'Better keep to the brushes,' said Tommy to the drummer.

The room was a mess by now. Bottles littered the floor, and it was unbearably stuffy from the large sweaty bodies crowded together. But music has the unique power of lifting us from our surroundings, helping us not to forget, but to transfigure them. I remember Monsieur Yepanchin's apartments – the dingy garret of a tumbledown house in Holborn – presenting a scene of unbelievable squalor. He was addicted to tobacco, and since he never opened the windows on account of the noise from the street, the place was pervaded by a truly sickening stale stench. The floor, and every other flat surface, was carpeted with sheets of music. Yet when I played there, with Monsieur Yepanchin accompanying me on the harpsichord, bending his long neck around every now and then to glance at me, it became a kind of palace. The music with which he filled the room seemed to push the walls back to create a spacious hall. And when Monsieur Yepanchin played a rippling scale on the harpsichord, it was as though the grime-stained casements had been flung open and a fresh breeze were blowing through.

Some hours must have passed as I sat on the floor with a bottle between my legs, drowsily listening to the music. Then the door was opened a second time. Now there stood before us a beautiful young woman. She was somewhat darker than Tommy – not bronze, but the shade of a dark wood. She leant lightly against the frame of the door and listened to the music with an almost disdainful smile. At its conclusion, she applauded.

'You guys are getting better, you know that?' she said. 'Pity you don't smell as sweet as you play.' She moved across the room to open the window, then turned around and surveyed us. Her glance rested on me.

'I haven't seen you here before,' she said.

'He's new here,' said Tommy. 'John Field's his name. This is May, my sister.'

'What you doing here, Mister Field?'

'He doesn't know,' said Tommy for me. 'Says he plays fiddle, so I'm gonna check him out. See if we can use him.'

'Where you from, Mister Field?'

'Yeah, where you say you're from, John?'

'England.'

Tommy was thoughtful for a moment. 'No, I don't know that.'

I smiled to myself.

'What's the joke, Mister Field?' asked May. 'Tommy say something funny?' She was smiling at me, looking at me steadily.

'Ah, leave him be,' said Tommy. 'He's all right.'

'Matter of fact,' continued May, ignoring her brother and addressing me, 'I've never heard of it either. That mean you're gonna laugh at me too?'

For a moment I was utterly crestfallen. 'I'm afraid,' I said, 'I'm afraid I don't know . . . madam.'

She laughed. 'Well, perhaps you'd better start thinking about it, Mister Field.' With that she disappeared from view down the corridor.

There was a pause. The guitar player coughed politely, and Tommy gave a low whistle.

'I shouldn't worry too much about May,' he said. 'I'm sure she didn't intend any offence. She's just got a sharp tongue. And she's maybe a bit suspicious. You know how things are.'

But of course I didn't know how things were. The episode cast me into considerable gloom, and even the resumption of the music failed to cheer me. I meditated on how much of a stranger I was in this place, and how irretrievable now seemed my mad decision to leave the ship and come here. Perhaps it had been a terrible, terrible mistake.

But my worries gradually eased. May put her head round the

door and asked if I expected to stay for supper. I looked to Tommy.

'Yeah,' said Tommy, 'he'll be staying.' She disappeared again, and he solicitously gave me another bottle of beer. 'Hey, cheer up,' he said. 'Say, we've got just the number for John here. Let's play "It's All Right Here For You".'

It was getting dark. The light was fading from the window. I was very tired by now, and everything around me was beginning to take on a dream-like aspect. Tommy's mother came in, and we were introduced. She was blacker than her children, rotund, with a distant and weary smile. She stood listening to the music for a long time, gazing at her son with a kind of helpless pride and swaying gently backwards and forwards on her enormous hips. A single bright light blazed from the ceiling. I watched the drummer's thick arms pump up and down onto the drums, the bass fiddler's long, thin face, eyes closed, twitch nervously. For a while I was frightened by the strangeness to me of it all.

May came in and said that it was time to eat. The drummer, the bass fiddler and the guitarist packed up their instruments and filed out of the door. May led the way along the dingy corridor, reeking of the smells of cooking, to the kitchen.

Eldridge was sitting morosely at the table, swigging on a bottle. He was drunk.

'At last,' he said. 'I've been waiting on my dinner for half an hour.'

'Now don't get like that, Eldridge,' said his mother as she shuffled over to the stove. 'Tommy was just playing to us. There's no harm in that.'

'I don't know why you bother with those old tunes. You should check out the stuff they're playing downtown these days. Man, that's real.' He snapped his fingers a couple of times and took another swig from his bottle. When he saw me, he took the bottle from his mouth and raised it. 'Ah, here's our bum from the railroad. How've you been getting on with my crazy brother?'

'He's certainly a very fine musician,' I replied.

Tommy winked at me as we settled ourselves around the table.

'Shit, you don't wanna bother with that grandpa music that he plays,' said Eldridge. 'I'll take you down one of the clubs some time, and you hear the shit they're putting down down there. Blow your mind. His stuff's been dead for years.'

'Bah, you're full of it,' said Tommy. 'Anybody could play that noise they put out down in the big clubs. Two chords and a lot of banging. You might as well go and listen to the trains rattling over the tracks.'

His mother giggled over at the stove. Eldridge turned on her. 'And why do you always take his side, Ma?'

'Boys, boys,' said May. 'This ain't a war.'

''Sides,' Eldridge continued, 'if that stuff's so easy to play, why don't you get down there and earn a bit of money for a change?'

'Because,' said Tommy quietly, leaning across the table towards his brother, 'I ain't gonna be nobody's Uncle Tom.'

His last words were almost lost in the commotion. Eldridge tried to grab Tommy across the table, and swung a fist at him. There was a crash from the stove as their mother slammed down a pan and burst into tears.

'Stop it, stop it, *stop it*!' she cried. 'Sometimes I wonder how I bear it. Tommy, I never want to hear you talking to your brother like that again, you hear me?' Silence. 'I said you hear me?'

'Yes, Ma.'

The mother was silent for a moment. Her head was shaking. She seemed confused and defeated.

'You wear me down, you do,' she said. 'I've gotta go upstairs and rest. May, you can call me in a while. And when I come back down I want to see some signs of civilised behaviour around here. I certainly don't know what this house is coming to.'

She left, while May busied herself at the stove. Tommy mumbled, 'C'mon, Eldridge, I'll get some more beers', and went out of the room. I witnessed all this in a state of acute embarrassment. As May put some plates on the table, she gave me a smile of reassurance. Tommy returned with some more beers. In his other hand he held a metal box.

'C'mon, Eldridge,' he said, 'put some tunes on.' He held the metal box out like an olive branch. Eldridge took it and switched it on. It made music, like those mechanical music boxes I remember so fascinating you. The sound was pleasant but automatic. At the stove, May's body was twitching. Eldridge got up and began to dance with her. The room was dim, with only the yellow light of a single lamp shafting across it. May bit her lower lip as she danced, and pressed her palms against the air. I became very aware of Tommy's presence beside me. He was eyeing his brother and sister as they danced.

'Never understood why May likes this stuff. She's a smart girl,' He took a swig of beer.

She certainly seemed to be enjoying herself. A sparkle had come into her eyes as she admired Eldridge's movements, then mimicked them outrageously herself. The music did have a somewhat hypnotic charm. I allowed my nerves to relax to it, and immediately wanted to talk. I turned to Tommy.

'Your sister is a remarkable young lady, but I think you're right as far as the music is concerned.'

'Damn right. Music's gotta be sweet. If it ain't sweet, it ain't music. You take this shit. A guy gets hold of riff, and just jams on that one riff. So there's no movement. This cornet player I know, Jake, you've gotta meet him, he says a tune's like a story, or a journey. He says that's what he thinks of when I'm playing. Like one time we were playing in this bar, and when it comes to my chorus he shouts out, "Tell me a story, Tommy my prince!" Well you can imagine, everyone had a good laugh over that. I mean they was already pretty whipped up, what with that cornet scorching the rafters for two hours. Boy was that good!' He paused to wipe his eyes. 'But that's what I'm getting at – a tune's like that story. You've got to *tell* it, with rhythm.'

And perhaps you are thinking, Father, that my telling of this story does not give you the facts of the case. (What was the function of those rail tracks? How does Eldridge's mechanical box produce its sounds?) You always used to divide the world into units to be weighed like the mounds of ripened corn in your weighing room. But, Father, a tale grows as a man grows. A melody does not tick by in equal measure like a clock; it is rhythm, not metre, and that is the life in music. So forgive me the facts.

The facts were before me: May was tiring, she danced less herself and spent more time admiring and laughing at Eldridge as he strutted up and down the confined space of the kitchen. Tommy was quite drunk by now. He gazed vacantly into the dim light and drummed out a rhythm with his fingers on the edge of the table. And for myself, the exertions of the past two days – the drink, the nervous strain of being plunged in among these strangers – they all combined in a great cloud of fatigue, through which I gazed, sentimentally, at May. She held a charming, easy sway over her warring brothers. With Tommy she was more respectful, perhaps distant, than with Eldridge. It was with the latter that she now bobbed and weaved on the grimy floor.

'I think Mister Field wants his dinner. You're looking hungry, Mister Field. You hungry?' The music had faded away, and she stood before me with her hands on her hips, smiling. Her dark blue singlet stuck to her skin where the sweat had run down between her breasts.

'Indeed yes . . . that is, whenever the meal is prepared, I would not want to impose . . .'

'Well, let's eat then,' she interrupted – fortunately, for my mind and jaws were so unhinged by my fatigue that I dread to think how I might have gabbled on. 'Always say what you want, Mister Field, else you'll never get anything. Ain't that right, Eldridge?'

Eldridge had thrown himself down on the seat beside me with a kind of whoop of exhilaration, as though to emphasise that had the music continued he would still be up there dancing. At May's words he leant enthusiastically across the table. 'Sure is,' he said. 'You get nothing for nothing in this world. A man's gotta look after himself, and he'll get what's due to him. Simple as that. If he don't do that . . .' – but May had turned from him almost as soon as she had asked the question, and deprived of his audience, he turned to me to complete it rather lamely – '. . . he won't get it.'

May had gone out into the corridor, where she leant over the stairs and shouted, 'Ma! You wanna come down now?' As she came back into the room she glanced at Tommy and said gently, 'Don't look so glum now, Tommy. I swear, keeping you two guys happy is like juggling.' Tommy smiled grudgingly. 'You gonna be playing in the parade tomorrow?'

'Guess so,' he replied.

'Well, I hope you don't just hang out with your buddies and get drunk. You'll join the CAU for a time, won't you?'

'Yeah, course I will. But the music comes first, you know that. That's the Civil Advancement Union,' he added to me. 'I stay out of that kind of thing. World's gonna go on like it goes on, and as long as they let me play my horn – and they ain't gonna bother to stop me – it don't worry me. Mind you, I think May's all right. I mean, they treat our people like shit, and someone should tell them, like *do* something about it.'

Eldridge had been listening to this at my shoulder, and when he had finished he added, 'The only way our people gonna help themselves is by getting off their asses and looking after themselves. That's the only way they're gonna get self-respect, be able to look after themselves.'

'Don't know why you say "they",' said Tommy. 'It's you as well.'

Their mother came in at that point and May put the plates of stew out on the table. Eldridge said to his mother, 'Mister Field here reckoned I was a slave.'

'Well, Mister Field certainly does have some interesting opinions,' she said.

I could feel May's curious gaze on me.

As we started eating the watery stew, Eldridge continued, 'Yeah, that's pretty off the wall. Like I told him, freedom's the name of the game here. I don't answer to no one.'

Tommy gave a low, mocking whistle.

'Ma,' said May, ignoring her brothers, 'I'll have to go down to Flanagan's office soon. We're okay for this month, but he's gonna hold us to the arrears.'

'Then we'll just have to see what we can work out,' replied her mother wearily.

'That's right,' put in Eldridge. 'If I get that promotion we'll be riding high. No problem.'

'I'm sure you'll do your best, honey,' said the mother. 'But as things are, we can't live on what might be.'

'If I might say something,' I said. 'Eldridge here was good enough to offer me assistance this morning when he found me in the hut by the railroad track. I am, as you know, a stranger in your land. He brought me back here, to your house, where Tommy offered me hospitality and gave me to understand that, if I so desired, I could lodge here for a time.'

The mother, to whom I was principally addressing myself, was looking at me intently, her face screwed up as though she could only follow what I was saying with the greatest concentration. A peculiar hush had fallen over the company; we had all stopped eating.

'Being a stranger here, and having, as it were, no foothold other than that which has been proffered by your good selves, I am most desirous to take up the offer and lodge here. But, and this is why I raise the subject in this context, I would not want to be the source of strain upon your resources. I do not have any of your local currency with which to pay for my keep, but I do . . . Perhaps if you could wait a moment I might show you.'

I got up from the table. The silence around the table still held, and the scraping of my chair on the stone floor seemed painfully loud. I went out through the dark corridor to the other room, where I had left my canvas sack. It was night outside now, but an odd yellow light from the lamps in the street flooded into the room. As I crouched down over the sack I looked at my hands. They too looked yellow and jaundiced, and for a moment I stared at them. This was the first time in that long day I had been alone, and in that brief moment as I fumbled in the sack I was filled with a melancholy consciousness of solitude. I thought back through the years to home. Visions of you, Father, flashed before me. I pulled out the purse and poured two coins into my yellow palm. An old couplet passed swiftly through my confused mind:

> *The Love of Gold, (That Jaundice of the Soul,*
> *Which makes it look so Gilded and so Foul)*

I returned to the kitchen, still with that sad sense of being utterly alone. The four black faces were turned blankly to me as I entered the room. Without a word I placed the coins on the table and sat down again. I felt too tired to speak.

Eldridge immediately took up the coins and weighed them in his hand.

'The universal language,' he said, grinning.

'You put those down, Eldridge, said his mother sternly. She looked at me. 'Well, Mister Field, I appreciate your gesture. You don't seem to have any place to go, and my sons seem to want you to stay. If I could I'd just wave my hand and say, "Now don't you worry about payment, Mister Field, cause you're a guest and no guest of ours pays." But unfortunately I can't do that. Don't think we haven't got pride. It's just that to express your pride in that way costs the kind of money we haven't got. So I'll thank you for your money and we'll consider it all settled.'

'You hang onto those for the moment, Mister Field,' said May quietly. 'We'll go down the bank and see what we can do with them.' She pushed the coins across the table towards me.

'Wait,' said Eldridge, snatching them up. 'I want a last look at these babies.' He turned them over and over lovingly in his pale palm. 'Beautiful.'

He gave me back the coins. The voices all tumbled together as another wave of drunkenness and fatigue swamped me. I half rose to my feet and said, 'If you'll excuse me, ladies and gentlemen, I think I might take the air . . .' Without quite knowing how, I was half way across the kitchen floor with Tommy at my side saying, 'Yeah, John, let's have us a smoke outside.'

The night was cool. There was moisture in the air. We sat on the steps outside the door and smoked. Tommy talked about music and about the parade that was to happen the next day.

'You'll meet this guy Jake I was telling you about. He's gonna be playing in the parade too. Then I'll take you down Lennox. There's a guy there got a violin you could use.'

Across the street there were lights burning in the houses, groups of people sitting around tables. Another snatch of something I had read folded over and over in my mind: *A man who looks out of an open window never sees as much as a man who looks at a window that is shut. What one can see in the light of day is always less interesting than what happens behind a pane of glass. In this black and lustrous pit lives life. Here life dreams, life suffers.*

For perhaps an hour we sat on the steps, until we began to feel the damp chill, then went back inside and up to a dark room, where I slept on a pallet on the hard floor, beneath rough woollen blankets.

I was woken next morning by shouting in the street.

'C'mon, you lazy no-good . . . gonna be late.'

From another direction came female laughter, and the click of heels on paving receded and then disappeared. I turned over, feeling the stiffness in my body. Tommy was asleep on another pallet a few feet away from me. The sunlight streamed in through the windows, and the air in the room was warm and fuggy with the smell of unwashed bodies. As I stared blankly at Tommy's long black back a door slammed downstairs and May shouted, 'Take care, Ma. Remember, I'll meet you on the corner of sixty-third and fourth at two. You just wait for me there and I'll be along.' Something inaudible was said in reply, and May laughed. Another door slammed. All was silent.

These sounds had woken me completely, the anticipation and excitement in the air making me restless. I dressed and went downstairs. The room in which I had slept was directly above that in which I had sat listening to Tommy playing on the previous day. I looked into this room now, found no one there, and passed down the corridor into the kitchen.

I discovered May and Eldridge. They stood facing each other. They were laughing, and May was trying to jam a cap further down onto Eldridge's head. Eldridge broke away from her and turned to me.

'What d'you think, John? How do I look?' He drew himself up like a soldier standing to attention. 'It's my uniform for the parade.'

May was standing beside him, smiling. Her eyes darted backwards and forwards between myself and her brother.

I looked him up and down for a moment. 'Excellent,' I said, and clicked my heels together as though I were a soldier too. Eldridge relaxed his stance.

'You want some coffee, Mister Field?' said May.

She poured some from a pot on the stove, and the three of us sat around the small table. This room, being at the back of the house, hardly caught the sun through its tiny window. It was so gloomy that even now, in the morning, the lamp that hung from the ceiling was lit. The silver badge that now adorned Eldridge's cap was caught in the strange yellow glow from this lamp, and twinkled brightly against the drab surroundings. It was the principal item in his 'uniform', for otherwise he was wearing the same as he had been the previous day. His leggings, however, had been washed and starched.

'This parade's gonna blow your mind, John,' he said. 'Shit, those hands and cheerleaders: they really go for it. I mean, *go for it*. Bet you don't have stuff like that in . . . where d'you say you were from?'

'England.'

'Yeah, that's right. Well, this is unique. Shit, I wish I was seeing it for the first time. Not that it ain't good even when you've seen it before. I'm gonna be marching with the company banner. First coloured man to carry the company banner in the history of the parade, Joe was telling me yesterday. Looks like being ay one okay for my promotion. Junior Engineer, then Engineer, then Assistant Chief Engineer. Whoooosh!' – the palm of his hand described an upward curve – 'I'm taking off, man. Reaching for the stars.'

There was a pause. The three of us, hunched across the table, were caught by silence. Eldridge stared at me, a smile stretched across his face and a sparkle of enthusiasm in his eyes. His speech hung in the air, unanswerable. I looked down at the table, then at May. She was watching me with interest. Meeting my gaze, she raised her eyebrows and frowned, as if to say, 'He's not going to change, so we can only respect his folly.' I looked back at Eldridge and found him in the same posture, still smiling.

'Man,' he continued. His voice had gone quiet, almost dreamy. 'Those flags, those uniforms. It's gonna knock you out.'

His voice jolted me. It was a strange moment. I felt I had missed the rhythm of the conversation.

'We all get the day off work today,' said May. She leant back in her chair. 'Everyone has a holiday.'

'Do you work?' I asked her.

She laughed. But it was not a hard laugh.

'Everyone has a holiday, everyone works,' she said. 'I work in an office downtown . . .'

'It's a damn good job, too,' Eldridge added to me.

'. . . Eldridge works on the railroad . . .'

'John's been down there. That's where we met.'

'. . . and Ma does cooking and cleaning for a white family. She's got the worst deal. They live right out in the suburbs. So she's gotta get up at six in the morning to get the train out there. She's not back till eight at night. She's been working for that family fifteen years now.'

May's tone was flat and matter-of-fact. The light above her head burned without flickering. It caught her black, curly hair, and her hair seemed to cast back from within its darkness, like a spread of oil in sunlight, a sheen of a thousand colours.

'And Tommy don't do nothing,' said Eldridge.

May sighed, and looked at him.

'He's playing in the parade, isn't he?' she said. 'It ain't just a holiday for him, like it is for us.'

'He'll just be fooling around,' said Eldridge. 'That's nothing. I'll be carrying the banner for the company.'

'Let's hope the company's grateful,' said May.

'What do you mean, grateful?' said Eldridge scornfully.

'All I mean is that you seem like you're hell-bent on pleasing the company, so I hope the company takes some notice and shows it's pleased with you.'

'What kind of crap is that?' Eldridge screwed up his face. 'Grateful? Pleased? Just like a woman. You're talking about *business*.' He stood up. 'C'mon then, John,' he said, 'let's hit it. I've gotta get my place on that banner.'

'Certainly, Eldridge,' I said, hesitating, 'only I did say to Tommy that I would accompany him, and I fear he's still asleep.'

A look of frustration and annoyance passed across Eldridge's face. 'Shit, you don't wanna waste time waiting around for that bum,' he said. 'Could be all day before he gets up.'

'That's why Mister Field should stick around here,' said May. She sat with her hands in her lap, smiling at Eldridge and myself. For a moment she reminded me of her mother.

'He's gotta make sure "that bum" gets up and goes to the parade.'

Eldridge stood over us silently.

'C'mon, Eldridge,' said May. She got up and turned towards the door, 'I'd better get you down there on time, else they might not start without you.'

'Yeah, well, I'll see you later,' said Eldridge from the doorway. May turned round too. 'You make sure Tommy makes it down there,' she said.

When the door onto the street had slammed and they were gone, I stood up to stretch my legs. May had extinguished the lamp that hung from the ceiling on her way out. Now there was only the light from the window. I stepped over to it and raised myself on tiptoe to look out. Behind the house was waste land like that beside the tracks. The sun shone on rubble, on rubbish, and on the green plants that grew up through it all. Across on the other side of the wasteland were three enormous buildings. They were grey slabs, like tombstones, punctured by small, mean windows. Overhead, clouds raced across the sky. But over there on the horizon it was clear, and the grey slabs stood out starkly against the wide blueness. The scene was unpeopled.

I turned away. The house was dark and cold, and I wanted Tommy's company. As I made my way up the stairs, I heard the wind that blew across the waste land rattle a window. The house was like a silent husk.

Tommy was lying luxuriously on his pallet when I entered his room. He was staring at the ceiling, with his hands clasped behind his back. Without moving, he glanced at me down the length of his body. The street outside was eerily quiet.

'So what's new, John?' he said.

I didn't understand.

'What you been doing?' he said.

'I've been talking to May and Eldridge,' I said. 'May wanted me to make sure you got to the parade in good time.'

Tommy grinned. 'Those guys. If they was dying they'd be worrying about whether they was going to be late for the next world. I say you've gotta let things fall into place.' He began humming a tune.

I walked over to the window and looked out. Why is it that while looked at objectively clouds are the same everywhere, we infuse them with the spirit of a place? These looked wild, moving quickly across the sky as though they might fly apart like shoots that have bolted. You'll dismiss such questions: either something is a true fact, in which case it may be discussed, or it is not, and may not. But whence do the errors arise? Perhaps from the very clouds themselves, the 'infusive force of Spring on Man', as the poet writes.

The passage of the clouds was broken by the rooftops and, in the further distance, by great metallic towers that glinted in the sunlight. The houses across the street were substantial and perhaps once of some standing, but they had fallen into considerable disrepair. Masonry had crumbled from the façades. Plants grew up between the steps and, in one case, shot from a smashed ground-floor casement.

I turned around. Tommy had dressed, and was sitting on the mattress smoking some tobacco.

'Well,' he said, 'I guess we'd better go.'

On the way we picked up Tommy's horn, and some bread from the kitchen. Outside, the street was deserted, save for two elderly Africans. We set off in the same direction as them. Tommy blew a few notes on his horn as we walked, and grinned at me.

'We'll catch the parade at the corner of fourth,' he said. 'That's where the viewing stand is. You know, like where all the politicians and the mayor and shit hang out. The poor suckers in that parade spend the whole fucking year getting together the banners and costumes and floats and shit, and all so those stuffed shirts can look at it for thirty seconds. It's the craziest shit you'll ever see.'

In the distance I could now hear music – trumpets and drums – and the roar of a vast crowd. Other people were hurrying along the streets in the same direction as ourselves, drawn to the noise like water sucked down a hole. Tommy seemed unperturbed by the mounting excitement around him. He strolled at an easy pace, swinging his horn in his hand and chatting all the while.

'. . . course I'm in what you might call the unofficial part of the parade, that's all the no-goods and loafers who tag on at the end' – he laughed – 'and you can bet the mayor and shit aren't gonna bother staying around to check *us* out!'

I barely heard what he was saying, such was my curiosity as to the source of the noise. The buildings on either side had grown larger now; the roar of the crowd rolled towards us as though down an enormous steep-sided gorge. The sound put me in mind of ancient Rome. It was as though we were going to the amphitheatre for an exhibition of blood.

'Well, shit,' said Tommy. We had turned a corner into the full blast of the crowd's roar, and were faced with a wall of backs. 'Now you stick close behind me and I'll get you through here.' Tommy started pushing a way through the crowd saying, 'Medical emergency . . . make way please, ladies and gentlemen . . . we have a situation here . . . c'mon, please make way . . . this is an emergency medical situation . . . thank you . . . please make way . . .' Miraculously, the crowd let us through, some of them even bullying those in front officiously to make a space through for us. When we had made it to the front, and had moved along the street to avoid the retribution of those we had deceived, Tommy grinned at me with delight.

'Now that's what I call free enterprise,' he said.

The crowd lined both sides of a broad street. Opposite us was a scaffold supporting a platform, on which sat a row of gentlemen in thick coats and hats. Beyond that was a park; the fresh spring leaves of the trees swayed in the breeze over the heads of the dignitaries. The platform was festooned with striped flags, all carrying a motif of stars in one corner. Down the middle of the street marched a troop of young girls waving sticks and flags. They wore short trousers and loose vests like the woman on the beach, but these were decorated with the same stripes and stars as the flags. As they kicked their legs in the air and flung up their sticks, the crowd let out a great roar. The girls were an extraordinary mixture of physical types: Europeans, Africans, Chinese, Japanese, Arabs. But they were given a powerful identity by their flimsy costume and by the strict step that they kept to the massed drums behind. Occasionally, in perfect unison, they would execute an intricate manoeuvre of the body, and as they drew level with the viewing stand they turned their heads in salute.

'See the mayor slobbering up there?' Tommy shouted in my ear. 'He's probably wet his pants by now.'

After the serried ranks of young girls, and the massed drums that drove them on, came a large cart somewhat dingily decked out with plants and a large model of a wooden shack. A woman in a pretty floral dress sat in front of the shack over a camp fire, and, nearby, two small children in similar costume danced around in a circle. Above them fluttered a banner that read, WE CELEBRATE OUR PIONEER HERITAGE. The crowd clapped politely as it passed. Those further up were already cheering the arrival of another large band. A blaring fanfare of trumpets swirled up between the immensely tall buildings, and then the very ground seemed to shake to the answering hammer of drums. The bandsmen swaggered arrogantly down the street in their bright scarlet costumes, swinging their instruments from side to side as they blasted out their stiff, four-square march tune. This band was merely a prelude, an advance guard, to another troop of girls, some two hundred strong, all leaping and flinging their sticks about. Behind them came the banner of the railroad company, carried by, among others, Eldridge.

'Yo, Eldridge,' cried Tommy in great excitement. 'Looking good, man, hey, man! Yo! Eldridge!' Tommy was jumping up and down and waving, but Eldridge, marching in the middle of a line of five men, who each carried a pole of the banner, did not notice him. The men stared ahead with grim seriousness. The banner they carried read, UPTOWN AND SUBURBAN RAILROAD CORPORATION INC.

Tommy was in a fever of excitement and frustration at not having caught Eldridge's attention. 'Yo, Eldridge, man,' he shouted, and, handing the horn to me, dashed out into the street to greet his brother. But as soon as he was in among the marchers, his arm was grabbed as he ran past, and he was swung violently around. Two of the marchers leapt on him, and at the same time a man in a blue uniform ran out from the crowd wielding a stout stick. He beat Tommy down with this, and, helped by the two marchers, dragged him to the side of the street. Tommy was shouting and protesting all the while. The marchers' fists rained down as he struggled and kicked beneath them. They left him in a heap at the side of the street and hurried back to their places in the march. The whole thing seemed to be over in but a moment, and by the time I reached him through the laughing crowd, Tommy had picked himself up off the ground.

'Fucking rednecks,' he said as he dusted off his trousers. 'Jesus wept, I was only going to say hi to my brother.' His lips were pursed with the effort of holding back the tears of pain and humiliation that pricked his eyes. Blood trickled from a cut on his left temple, and there was heavy bruising about his right eye.

He managed a smile. 'Is my horn okay?'

'A small compensation, but it is,' I replied.

'Yeah, well, I guess that's something. C'mon, let's get out of here.'

I handed his horn back to him, and we started walking back along the crowd. People shouted at us as we passed to get out of the way and off the street. Tommy gradually regained his spirits, to the extent that a couple of times, by way of reply, he aimed an insolent blast of his horn at the sea of hostile faces. Once we had to scamper on quickly when a group of men threatened to grab us and drag us into the crowd.

In the opposite direction came more uniformed marchers, more drums, more deafening fanfares. The initial glory of the parade had faded, the attack on Tommy had made me somewhat nauseous, and I now trudged behind him wishing that the whole thing were over. I think even you, Father, with your love of ceremony and pomp, might have found it too rich a feast. There is but a difference of degree between the desire to impress and the desire to beat into submission.

And so I was all relief when it became clear that we were reaching the end of the parade, as the troops became smaller, less opulent, and diluted by elements of the crowd who had elected to follow the parade. Suddenly I caught sight of May. She was with a motley bunch who were marching beneath a banner that read 'Civil Advancement Union', and beneath, 'Freedom Justice Unity'. I pointed her out to Tommy.

'Jesus,' he said, wiping a trace of dried blood from his temple, 'I don't want her seeing me like this. Here, you tell her I had to go find the band. Go on, go talk to her. We'll touch base later.' With one hand he pushed me towards the marchers, and with the other waved farewell. Then he disappeared into the crowd.

The CAU banner had already passed during the course of this transaction. I had to hurry along the road to catch up with it again, and then push my way through the ranks of marchers to May. At last, I reached her.

'Excuse me. Miss . . .' I realised I didn't know her surname. 'May . . . if I may.' A tall white man walking at her side roared with laughter.

'A comedian! Sounds like the title of a corny song.'

A shudder of resentment passed through me at being laughed at by a stranger. And then immediately it occurred to me that on the previous evening May had laughed at me and I had not minded, indeed I had revelled in it. Now she was smiling at the man's remark, and I wished she was smiling at me. She had given me only one brief glance as I arrived, somewhat breathless, beside her.

'Tommy sends his apologies,' I said, 'But he says he has to find the other members of the band.'

'Oh well, I guess it was kinda inevitable,' she said equably.

'Actually,' I continued, to make myself more interesting, 'we experienced a somewhat unpleasant incident. Tommy was injured by some men in the march.'

'What happened?'

I proceeded to give them an account of Tommy's intervention in and ejection from the march. The gentleman at her side snorted with indignation, while May listened gravely.

'Is he hurt bad?' she asked.

'No. He's quite recovered. The wound was superficial.'

'Hell, those guys are fascists,' cried the tall gentleman. 'If I could get my hands on them I'd . . .' He turned to me. 'You know why they did that to *him*?' Looking me up and down for the first time, he added, 'Where did you say you were from?'

'Oh sorry,' said May. 'Mike S——, this is John Field, from England.'

'Yeah, England,' the man continued. 'Well, it's the colour of his skin. It's because he's black.'

May laughed, but wildly and somewhat sadly. 'He ain't even black,' she said. 'He's coffee bean.'

'Yeah, but he's still *black*, that's what counts. To those guys.'

Mr S—— was older than myself and, in point of fact, immensely tall. As he talked to May he had to stoop down to catch anything she might say. His long legs covered the ground quickly. And, as he was walking at the front of the group, he could set his own pace. The other marchers had to hurry along to keep up with him. His manner was, as they say in polite circles, *gauche*. Much of the time he talked to himself.

'Thing that'll surprise you, John,' he was saying, 'is the *pace* of change here. Things are moving. It's amazing. I've been heavily involved with the CAU for three years now, and it's amazing what we've achieved. I really feel we're reaching out to people and touching them in a very special way. Those guys that beat up on Tommy are on a loser. They belong in history, in the dustbin.'

As he talked, he waved to the small crowd that had lingered after the main parade had passed. Most of the people had dispersed, and many of them could now be seen making their way across the park that lay on one side of the street. The parade was dissolving, like an essence, into the great sea of the city. I had tired of the tall man's prattling, and was listening to other, more distant, sounds. Up ahead one of the uniformed bands thudded into the distance amidst muffled applause. But from behind me came a new strain, a liquid stream of notes that was lost and caught again on the breeze.

'That'll be Tommy's band,' said May. She had been looking at me, and had heard what I was listening to. 'Guess he found them after all.'

The tall man talked on. His voice jarred against the wafts of music – '. . . that was when I first started out in alternative politics, and things were really basic then. We're a lot more sophisticated now . . .'

'Say, Mike,' May interrupted him, 'I've gotta run now. I told my brother I'd check out his band and stuff. Catch you at the meeting on Tuesday. Okay?'

'Sure thing. Have fun now.'

She turned to me. 'Don't suppose Mister Field would be interested in some music?'

'That would be lovely,' I replied. We walked away together.

'I thought the obligations between yourself and your brother ran in the other direction,' I commented when we were alone. 'Tommy was meant to join your march.'

She laughed. 'Well, you know, Mister Field, things sometimes don't turn out like you expect them to. Besides, I could tell you were itching to get away.' She gave me a wry smile. 'I do hate to see a man suffer.'

The musicians were just in view now, the sun glinting on their instruments. As the music enveloped us, May snapped her fingers and put a little skip into her step. Then when we were closer she put two fingers into her mouth and let forth a penetrating whistle.

'Yay, Tommy. Play that thing,' she cried.

There were six pieces in this band: a drummer, who played on a single drum slung from his neck; the guitarist of the previous day, an enormous bass brass instrument; a trumpet; a trombone; and Tommy. Tommy walked between the trumpeter, who was large and very dark, and the trombone. The march they played had swing and bounce. It was hard to walk in time to it, for the syncopations weakened the knees and made one dance. Strange scales cascaded from Tommy's horn, while the trombone egged him on with evil slides and snarls. The cornet had a full blazing tone. He could start notes with a crisp 't', with a growl, or with a swooshing glissando that seemed to wind the music up to a stratospheric pitch.

'That trumpet there,' said May in my ear, 'he's about the only trumpet in town that'll play with my brother. Tommy's too hot for the others – they say he plays too loud, takes the trumpet's part. But everyone knows it's just that he's too hot for them. He blows them off the stand. Our man there, he's the only one'll take Tommy on. They play up a storm together!'

'Is his name Jake?' I asked, remembering my conversation with Tommy the previous evening.

'Right in one, Mister Field. You're getting pretty knowledge-able.' She took my arm and drew me to the side of the road so that we would not be in the way of the band as they passed. 'You'll get to meet Jake. Tommy hangs out with him a lot. I never seen a man down as much liquor as that Jake does. Watching that man drink, you don't know whether to laugh or cry. Just about everybody knows Jake. He plays a lot of trumpet.'

The musicians shuffled along, jerking their instruments from side to side. Around them walked some two dozen Africans, who clapped and yelled encouragement at the musicians. The trumpeter kept his trumpet pointcd upwards, as though trying to feed the sky with his notes. At one point a scorching blast brought forth a flock of pigeons from a tree at the edge of the park. The Africans laughed and cheered at this.

Most of the crowd that had cheered the parade had been European-looking, and a few of them lingered on now, staring without interest at the band. Tommy's outfit was clearly not considered a proper part of the parade. I was reminded of those old religious processions where the clerical dignitaries were followed by members of the populace, aping them. Only Tommy and his companions were aping no one; there was a fierce pride in their playing.

The band and its followers soon turned off the wide street on which the parade had taken place and headed up towards the area where the Africans lived. We followed them. The buildings changed from the ugly glass and metal towers that blocked out the sky, to terraces of large brown houses with big wide steps up to the front door and iron railings. Children played on these steps, and outside some houses there stood groups of young African men, who scowled at those walking by. Altogether, there were more people on the streets here than down nearer where the parade had been held. People spilled out of the shops and coffee-houses when they heard the music, and stood blinking in the sunlight as we passed. They presented a great array of colours, from the deep purple black I had seen on the Gold Coast, through Tommy's coffee colour, to the palest of yellows. Again, some had broad-lipped African noses, while others, equally dark, had long straight ones like Hindoos. Their clothes were various, from rich dark suits that followed the leg and gripped the ankle, to threadbare dresses and smocks.

'I guess you can't see many of your "slaves" here, Mister Field?' said May.

'Indeed not . . . I do hope I didn't cause any offence by my remark. It was a misunderstanding. You see, from my previous experience . . .'

'C'mon, don't get all defensive on me. Besides, I guess there might be different kinds of slavery. That's what Tommy always says, anyway. That's why he won't get mixed up in the CAU. What's the point in fighting to get a stinking job like Eldridge has got, he says, just so we can get ordered around by whites like we were back on the plantations? Well, that's what he says, but I don't think he's got any better answers.'

'Well, he's got his music,' I said. 'I suppose that's something.'

'That ain't nothing. You should know better than that, Mister Field. You said you were a musician. Music don't solve your problems. It makes new ones, or makes the ones you got get worse. But we keep on doing it, that's the crazy thing. Guess that's the beauty of it. There, that's what your music does for you.'

Laughing, she pointed at the musicians. They had stopped playing and were standing outside an ale-house. A boisterous crowd had gathered around them, and from inside the house they had been handed a large jug, which they were passing around. Jake, true to his reputation, was taking a long draught of the brown liquid. He was cheered wildly.

Tommy saw us and came running over. 'Hey, you guys,' he shouted as he was half way across the street, narrowly dodging one of the carriages that hummed up and down the road. 'Good to see you, May,' he said breathlessly when he reached us. 'You guys gotta come in here with us and have a taste.

'We're jacking this marching stuff in now,' he continued as he ushered us across the street. 'We ain't even getting paid for this. I mean *come on* – is that anyway for a musician to behave? So we figure we'll kick back in here for a while.'

'Okay, but I can't stay long,' said May. 'I've got to meet Ma. I'm sure Mister Field'll keep you company. He's been digging your music.'

'I've found our man with the fiddle, John,' said Tommy. 'He's over here in the bar.'

The ale-house was one long thin room that stretched away from the street frontage. Down one side of it ran a bar from which were delivered the drinks by an important gentleman in a white apron. The crowd which had gathered outside had most of them dispersed, but a few had come in with the musicians and were now standing around Jake, who was playing upon the keyboard.

Tommy sat May and I down at a nearby table and went to the bar for some refreshment. When he returned, May quizzed him about the incident at the parade and examined his injuries.

But my attention was fixed upon Jake, whom I had not as yet examined at close quarters. He was broad in the chest and six foot tall, with a solid oblong head topped by greying curly hair. He was, I now saw, a good deal older than Tommy or myself, being about fifty or fifty-five. He had a long thin nose, but was as black as pitch. Well spaced on either side above this nose was a pair of small but sparkling and vivacious eyes. As he played, these were turned on the audience in various amusing attitudes of surprise, rapture, and humorous complicity. His music rolled along, with the beat pounded out by the left hand and the right blocking in the tune. He sang with a voice that was croaky in the bass and surprisingly tender in the upper register. The stomping rhythm and the clownish inflections of his voice made for a compulsive show.

When he had finished playing, Jake worked his way through the back-slapping crowd to our table. May interrupted her conversation with Tommy to greet him. 'Jake, you see what those assholes done to my brother?'

For a moment his smile faded, and he sat down at the table. Then he leant across the table, and holding Tommy's chin delicately between the fingers of one hand, examined the bloodied face.

'Least his chops is okay, ain't they?'

Everybody around the table laughed. But Jake, as though he had not been properly understood, went on, 'Well, that's what counts, isn't it? The boy's still got his chops: he can do his thing.' Only then did his deadpan expression break into a grin.

'You guys just take everything lying down,' said May with exasperation.

'Not you, May,' said Jake, 'I don't reckon I could take you lying down.'

'Too right you couldn't, old man, and if you tried you wouldn't be getting up afterwards.'

'Hahaha.'

The banter flew back and forth across the shiny table-top. I looked round at the brown and black faces that filled the bar, then down at my hands resting in my lap.

'Who's our pink-faced friend here?' asked Jake.

'This is John Field. He plays fiddle, don't you, John?' said Tommy.

'Yes.'

'That's all right,' said Jake. 'Welcome to our Pleasure Palace here.' His arm swept across the room.

'Yeah,' said Tommy, 'we gonna fix him up with a fiddle.

'Well, Peewee's your man. Hey, Peewee!' Jake shouted across the room.

'Yeah,' said Tommy, 'that's what I was telling him.'

'Hey, PEEWEE! Yeah, you, Peewee. Come on over here a moment will you.'

A small thin man slid off his stool at the bar and came over to our table.

'Peewee, how you doing, man?' said Jake. 'Listen, this is . . . what you say your name was?'

'John Field.'

'Yeah, this is John Field.' The thin man looked at me for a moment, then immediately cast his eyes down as though drawing a veil between us. 'He reckons he can play a bit of fiddle. You got your fiddle with you?'

'Yeah.'

'Well, go get it. Let's have some tunes around here.'

Peewee mumbled something.

'Sure,' said Jake. 'Hey, barman,' he shouted to the important man in the white apron, 'get this guy a beer.'

We watched as Peewee disappeared to the back of the bar.

'You don't wanna mind Peewee,' Tommy whispered to me. 'He's kinda simple you know, a country boy. Been in the city a long time, but he ain't got around to dealing with it yet. Say, Jake, what's he do with himself, Peewee? Guess he just sits over there at the bar and waits for suckers to buy him drinks?'

'Guess.'

Peewee returned with his violin, took the beer that had been bought for him from the table, and handed me the violin. It was rather a battered instrument; most of the varnish had been worn off the back, and a large patch on the belly was also bare. The bow was most curious, the wood being bent concavely towards the hairs.

'C'mon then, Mister Field,' said May gaily, and she took a sip of beer. 'Let's hear what you're made of.'

I stroked the bow across the open strings. They were in tune with each other, but pitched higher than I was used to. I ran my fingers silently over the gut strings for a moment, thinking what to play. It had, of course, been a good long time since last I had picked up a violin. My fingers felt small and stiff. But I placed my third finger on the A string, raised my bow to the frog, and began Corelli's 'La Follia'. After the second variation I stopped and looked round at my audience. Tommy seemed to start when I looked at him.

'Shit, that was sweet, John,' he said. 'Real sweet. Don't you reckon, Jake?'

'Pretty good,' said Jake, raising his eyebrows.

'Well, I got to be leaving you guys,' announced May. 'Ma'll be waiting for me.' She smiled at me. 'It's all right, John, it isn't your music driving me away.'

She left, swallowed up by the crowd that milled around the entrance to the bar. When I looked back to my companions I found Jake's eyes fixed on me.

'Say, you gotta bass line for that tune?' he asked.

'Indeed, there is a ground bass that runs through all the variations.'

'Well, c'mon over here and show us.'

As we got up to go over to the keyboard, I heard Jake say to Tommy, 'Yeah, I reckon we might be able to use this guy.' I felt a small thrill of pride run through me when he said that.

The keyboard had a fine resonant tone, like the striking of bells. I demonstrated the simple bass line, and Jake repeated it over at one hearing.

'Of course it is a figured bass,' I explained. 'To indicate the harmonies, you understand. But to save my soul, I'm afraid I cannot recall the figures.'

Jake laughed. 'Don't you worry about figures. I like to work out my own chords. You just go fetch the fiddle and we'll play it through.'

As I left him, Jake laughed again and shouted after me, 'And leave the soul-saving to God, Mister Field.' There were one or two light-hearted 'Amens' from those standing around.

When I returned, Jake and I played through the whole of 'La Follia' – the theme and all the variations. Towards the end, Tommy joined in as well. Jake was a most sympathetic accompanist, catching immediately the mood and tempo of each variation. His harmonies were somewhat richer than those I was used to; they had about them something of a dark, mournful humour. But his syncopations of the quicker episodes had a lively spirit. And Tommy's embellishments of the last two variations made the nicest counterpoint.

For my own part, I was transported back to that time in my life when I first learnt the piece under the guidance of my teacher, Monsieur Yepanchin. For nothing can excite the brain like music and even the musician as he plays is filled with a million passing thoughts and images. It was in the spring of my eleventh year, I remember, that you first took me to London to play for him.

Every spring you made your trip to London for business, and to call upon the acquaintances you had acquired at court. The spring was, for me anyway, the beginning of an annual journey. For the leaves and grasses at that season were a light, clear green. They were washed by showers, and I loved to follow them as they grew to the lush dark of August. That deep green of the late summer I associate with home; lying in the garden, on the narrow wooden bench you had had the coachman make, the overwhelming presence of the verdure, the broad leaves and delicate grasses focused my senses. There was a sanity about those days that I may have lost for ever. But the early spring always makes me think of that first journey in the carriage to London. The early spring was given to music. You took me to concerts at Westminster and Greenwich. For days my head was filled with Purcell and Boyce, Corelli and Handel. Portly with puppy-fat, filling out my baggy breeches, I stumped humming along the streets of London. And back at home in Cambridge I would return to practising my violin with an unhappy determination that worried both you and my mother. My efforts were spurred by images of the musicians at Westminster – the violinists moving as one, the whole ensemble caught in the graceful comradeship of creation.

Back in the strange ale-house surrounded by the Africans, I savoured once again the familiar feel of the strings beneath my fingers and of the bow balanced in my right hand; and I marvelled that out of this sensual solidity came music. As I leant into the violin and drew the bow across the strings it was as though I could distil the objects around me, the tables, the wooden floor, even the strange brown faces, – even as I had once distilled the familiar landscape of my room at home – into a single note.

On the last chord Tommy performed an intricate cadence, modulating through several keys as he climbed to the unearthly heights of his instrument, then falling down to a restful low note. There was applause from those immediately around us.

'You wouldn't think it's the same instrument that Peewee there plays, would you, Jake?' said Tommy.

'That's for sure. Hey, Peewee,' Jake shouted over to the bar again, 'c'mon over here and give us a tune. Get yourself a drink there and play us some blues.'

Peewee bought his drink and shuffled over to where we were standing around the keyboard. He was one of those men whom the cares of the world had aged prematurely; hard times had hollowed and scraped him like a dry bone. He took the violin from my hands without a word, shoved it gracelessly beneath his bristly chin, and began to play.

His manner of playing was different to mine in almost every respect. Even the way he held the instrument – grasping the bow crudely half way up its length and bunching the wrist of his left hand up against the neck of the violin – went against all I had been taught. But oh, that sound. I had never achieved that naked power. It seemed to me now that my music had always been precious and unreal, like fragile crystal glass. And now this music blew, smashing it to a thousand pieces. I resolved in future to attain that spirit myself.

Tommy and Jake began playing along with the violin. Tommy filled in the harmony with long soft notes below the violin, while

Jake provided a relentless, grinding rhythm in the bass. The dirge proceeded, and as I listened I began to understand all the music I had heard from Tommy and his companions in a new light. It was a strange, pure substance, as though in addition to earth, water, fire and air I had found a new, unknown element, or something infinitely old.

When they had finished playing, Tommy went off to the bar with Peewee to buy some more drinks. I sat down with Jake and related to him what I had been thinking about the music.

'Yeah, guess that's one way of looking at it,' he said dubiously, and took a swig of his drink. 'What you think of Tommy's horn? Pretty hot, eh?'

'Yes, very fine indeed.'

'Yeah it's good, a young guy like that playing the music. You know something? A guy like that could be playing down in them clubs downtown – the boom-boom music I call it – and he could be making a hundred bucks in one night. A hundred bucks. But he don't, 'cause he cares about what he does. Cares about the music. You heard the stuff the kids like to listen to down there?'

'I'm afraid I haven't, though Tommy's brother, Eldridge, has invited me to go to a club with him.'

'Yeah, well, you go listen to that shit and you'll see just what I mean. That stuff ain't even music, just a couple of chords pumped out by some machine as loud as possible. Who can play a real sweet tune on top of that? I'm too old for that scene anyway, been playing music too long. But Tommy there, he's young. They'd snap him up, eat him with fries they would. But he stays up here this end of town and plays the music. Beats me.' He laughed heartily, shaking his head.

The object of these considerations was in the middle of a raucous crowd gathered at the bar. As the light drained from the street outside, the ale-house filled with more and more black and brown men, until they were standing jammed together. Jake and I were sitting at a small table beside the large wooden cabinet that housed the keyboard, and every now and then the man standing closest to us would be almost pushed backwards onto our table. Friends greeted Jake as they made their way through the throng, glancing at me with curiosity. Jake was drinking heavily.

'Tell you something else,' he continued after a few minutes. 'We're both musicians. We can understand each other. Where I come from I knew this old guy played talking drums. Where my folks come from way before that, there was one of these drummers in every little town. These guys would talk to each other across the forest. This old guy I knew was one of the last could still do it, but he knew another old guy in the town over the hill who still played drums too. I can remember them sending messages to each other in the evenings. Man, they had a regular little network going there.' He smiled at me and shook his head again. 'Yeah, ain't it true. Music's straight from the devil's workshop.' He laughed.

His words evoked in me the ghostly, steaming days and nights on the African coast and in the West Indies. Always the heat, and the hostile, endless terrain.

'Are you from the West Indies?' I asked.

'Sure,' he said. 'I came here when I was a child. My dad was looking for work.'

I was on the point of asking him more, when Tommy appeared out of the crowd.

'Whole town's in here tonight,' he said, leaning across the table. 'Jones is over at the bar.'

'No kidding?' said Jake.

'Yeah, he's back from the sticks. Cool and full of talk. Says he got kicked outta the band for bringing some high yeller girl onto the bus one night.'

'Bringing himself back dead drunk, more like,' said Jake laconically. 'Couldn't keep his chops in order.'

'He's got Ed Davis with him. They want to talk you 'bout something.'

'Hell, suppose I'd better see what those low-lifers are up to.' He got up to go. 'I'll catch up with you another time, Mister Field.'

'Yes, it's been good to make your acquaintance.'

He pushed his way out through the crowd and towards the bar, his grey curly hair visible over the other heads.

'John, I don't wanna drag you away from this scene,' said Tommy, 'so I'll see you back at home. I've gotta go play my horn.'

'I think I'd better come back with you, if that's convenient. I don't really know where I am, or how to get back to the house.'

'Sure.' Tommy laughed.

Outside, the stars were obliterated by a wash of yellow light from the lamps which were strung up on high poles along the street.

'This is Lennox,' said Tommy. 'The main drag.'

We weaved up the street between groups of people who stood talking and looking around them as if waiting for something to happen. Their dark faces appeared sickly beneath the yellow lights. Some carried boxes like Eldridge's, and the same mechanical music blasted from the open doors of taverns. After some half a mile we crossed the street and turned left.

'This is hundred and thirtieth. We live just off this one further up. If you keep going up this one you get to the railroad track.'

We walked on in silence. This street was less crowded; only now and then were there people gathered on the steps that led up to each house. As we approached, they would stop talking and watch us steadily as we passed.

A right turn into a smaller street brought us home. The small house at the end of the short street was dark. But once inside, there was a glimmer of light from the kitchen at the back. May was sitting at the table reading a book. She put it down when we came in and leant back in her chair.

'Hi, you guys,' she said, with that unnerving smile. 'Have fun?'

Tommy flopped down into a chair. 'Yeah, okay. Shot the crap for a while, played some tunes. You know the scene.' He sighed deeply. 'Hell, I'm beat.'

'Yeah, Ma's tired. She's gone up to bed. Eldridge's down town some place with his buddies from work. How about you, Mister Field? Your fiddle-playing go down okay?'

'I think I acquitted myself reasonably.'

'Good for you, Mister Field.'

There was a long pause. The atmosphere was close; the stale

smells of old cooking hung in the air. I felt constricted by the tiny room, and longed to be out on the street again, in the cool night.

'Well, I guess I'd better go over some licks now,' said Tommy.

'I think I might take a walk around outside,' I put in, 'before retiring.'

May looked at Tommy sharply. 'You think he'll be okay?' she asked. Tommy shrugged. 'Listen, Mister Field. I'll come out with you, if that's okay. I'm getting kinda bored sitting here. I'll show you the park and the railroad and stuff.'

So May and I went out together. As we walked down the street to hundred and thirtieth, Tommy's horn could be heard starting a slow scale.

'Mister Field,' began May. 'I hope you won't think I'm being too protective. It's just that, well, there aren't too many white people live around here, and since you don't know your way around too well yet . . . well, I'd hate you to run into trouble straight away, seeing as that you've just arrived here.'

'Believe me,' I said, 'I do appreciate your concern. But thus far everybody has been most cordial.'

We turned right towards the railroad track when we came to hundred and thirtieth.

'Yeah,' May continued, 'I guess somehow they can tell you aren't the usual honky from downtown.' She stopped, and looked at me closely. 'You aren't, are you? I mean, you aren't some kind of trickster, are you, Mister Field?'

'No. I assure you that everything I told you was true.'

She frowned, looking me in the eyes searchingly. 'Well, I believed you. So did Tommy and Eldridge. That's why we took you in. You had no place to stay, didn't know anyone in town. Well that's something we can understand. Take that guy Peewee you met today. He was like you – arrived in town, didn't know his way around, didn't know anybody. Only he still hasn't got a foothold, probably never will now. Just clings to that bar like it was a life-raft. There are hundreds like him in this city. Thousands. Just like drops in the ocean. Most of them, they'll drift along till they die without no one noticing them. I guess you struck lucky early on.'

'I'm very grateful for all you and your family have done. To be sure, I don't know where I'd be without the help you've given me.'

She smiled, and reached out her hand to squeeze mine. 'Well, just so long as you're duly appreciative, Mister Field.'

We had turned into a small park. There were no yellow lamps here, just the white light of the moon. I could see the stars above. My mind raced back to the nights at sea when I would lie awake on the deck and look up at the night sky. The stars had been clearer then; here they were obscured, constricted, by buildings and by lights in the distance. Yes, it is only at sea that one can really see the stars. I looked around. There were ugly metal benches, paved paths, some trees, and a lawn from which nearly all the grass had been worn away. Across the ground were strewn pieces of paper and rubbish. Their whiteness seemed to glow in the dark.

'I guess there was something strange about you,' May was saying. 'Like you were an innocent. Yeah, an innocent.' She laughed. 'That must sound dumb.' She was silent for a few moments, then went on, 'Perhaps that's why Tommy gets on with you. He's an innocent too, only he ain't nobody's fool, like Eldridge is. Deep down, it's Eldridge that's the innocent one.' There was a long silence. 'Then, deep down, we're all innocent.'

At the other side of the park was the steep bank that sloped down to the waste land and the railroad tracks. We sat side by side on the grass. In the distance there was an unhuman roar, and a whistle shrieked into the night.

'Wish I was on that train,' said May quietly. 'Sometimes I wish I could just take off like that and go somewhere different.'

We were both looking out into the darkness. I could see nothing.

'I was the only one who finished high school,' she continued. 'Tommy and Eldridge both quit. I guess I was brought up to take things more serious than that 'cause I was a girl. I'd have liked to go to college, but there was no way I could do that. Ma kind of let me know that I had a responsibility. I don't remember my father. He went off somewhere else looking for work and Ma never heard from him again. That's all she's ever told me about it. I don't even know if Tommy and Eldridge've got the same father as me. I don't like to ask her about any of that. There's a whole lot of families like us in this neighbourhood. The men go off some place, to look for work maybe, and the women are left to bring up the children the best way they can. They don't hear from the father no more, 'cause he's got some other women by now in whatever city he's landed up in and if she's got no kids then he won't have to pay out so much. I didn't want to be used like that, so I kind of knew I had to get a job. I couldn't afford college. I had good grades from high school, so I got myself a job downtown as a secretary. But I kept on reading books and stuff, just like I really was at college. But reading ain't enough. Sometimes all education gives you is restlessness.'

'When I first arrived here,' I said, 'when Eldridge found me down there in the hut by the tracks, he called this the land of freedom. What did he mean by that?'

'Huh. That sounds like Eldridge all right. Well, I guess he's right, only it isn't as easy as he thinks. You see we're all from some place else. We've all shaken off our moorings – like you, Mister Field – or been torn away from them. That's a kind of freedom. It's a burden as well, that's what Eldridge don't realise. That's what makes him so innocent. It's a burden on your future, 'cause nobody owes you nothing. There are no debts to pay. You gotta fight every goddam inch. Freedom's not gonna fall into your lap. Our people aren't gonna get it till they stand up and demand it. That's why the CAU's important. None of us are gonna get anything without it. Shit, I'm talking to you like you were a meeting. Sorry. These things weigh on you.'

Below us, a mist lay over the railroad tracks. The air was tangible with moisture. We sat in silence for several minutes and I thought about what she had said. The words hung in the air, droplets of water. Freedom: the word was there, as tangible as the mist, but just as difficult to grasp and hold. My mind felt set adrift in a free-floating confusion; only the living presence of May beside me drew me back to the reality of the scene.

'I have always sought freedom by running away,' I began. 'I ran away from home at thirteen, and I've been escaping ever since. In just a few years I've seen half the world. I've dreamt of throwing off everything that ties us down – the circumstances of our birth, the age in which we live, even our own humours – and by some leap becoming free. But dreams are nothing. And I'm afraid that when I think on it, freedom is to me nothing more than that: a dream, an insubstantial thing. It is simply the absence of constraint, which is but a negative and a nothing.'

'Well, maybe that's where we're different,' she said, ''Cause to me it's as real as you sitting there next to me. More real.' She reached out and held my hand again. Her grip was warm and firm. 'It's all right, Mister Field,' she laughed. 'I'm just checking you're really there.'

The ground was damp. We got up and returned across the park to where the lamps cast their eerie yellow light. As we walked back to the house, May talked of her ambitions for the CAU, of the struggle to make freedom a reality. I listened, looking up through the yellow haze and trying to regain that clarity of the stars that I had lost.

We slipped quietly back into the house and said good-night. I found Tommy sitting on his pallet cleaning his horn with a rag. He greeted me with a wry smile.

'How were the trains?'

'Oh, we didn't see any. I think we heard one.'

'Hell,' he said, with a laugh. 'You can hear them from here. No need to go out there for that.'

'Well, it's pleasant just to wander abroad.'

Tommy shook his head. 'Beats me. You wanna beer?'

So before bedding down we shared a bottle of beer. Once, as if to prove Tommy's word, we heard a faint shriek disappear into the night. We slept.

These then, Father, were my first two days' experience of the strange land on which I had been cast ashore. I hope you have not found my narrative of them too exhaustive; I can imagine you tutting over it in irritation. 'Search out the facts of the case, boy,' you always used to tell me. You will be annoyed with me by now for not sifting out the salient points for the advancement of knowledge, for dredging up instead the whole messy and partial stuff of what I saw and heard from my first arrival on these shores.

I need no defence, of course. But should you require one, dutiful son that I am, I can provide it. For is it not first impressions that strike one most forcibly? Just as the lover rehearses a thousand times that pregnant moment when first sweet vows and kisses were exchanged; even so did every fleeting aspect of my introduction to this new country burn its mark upon my brain. Now there's a pretty argument for you to file away, Father.

Whatever the rights and wrongs of the case, my first two days in the city contained more interest and incident than the subsequent few – which were, in truth, a little dull. Tommy left for the 'sticks', where he and some other musicians were to put on a few performances; somewhat to my disappointment, he did not suggest that I accompany him. The next day, May took me out in the morning to change some of my gold coins for local currency. We walked to Lennox, but instead of turning right down the wide street, towards the bar where I had met Jake, we turned left. The weather was dull, the sky crowded with clouds the colour of musket barrels. Once or twice, a spot of rain brushed my cheek. May walked briskly through the crowds. I hurried along beside her.

'Here we are,' she said.

She was heading for a massive building that was set back from the road and raised, as if on a pedestal, to the head of a flight of imposing stone steps. As we climbed these steps, I raised my eyes to the thick Roman pillars that upheld the façade. The Africans around us fell silent as the portals loomed over them. But May remained unawed.

'This is the only bank in the neighbourhood,' she explained as we reached the top of the steps, 'and of course it's owned by whites. You want to save your money, you've gotta come here and give it to them. You got no choice.' Her voice rang out and echoed between the cold pillars.

The interior, a large domed chamber, was decorated in the most vulgar Italian style. There were more columns around its perimeter, wreathed in imitation gold leaf ivy, and above them naked cherubim blew trumpets at the ceiling. The Africans, in their coats and hats, looked isolated on the great expanses of the marble floor.

Two thirds of the way across the chamber was a partition, and a row of desks. Clerks sat behind the desks, and before them queued the Africans. We joined one of the queues and waited. When the Africans around us spoke to each other it was in a whisper, as though they were in church.

We reached the front of the queue. The clerk behind the desk was African. Her lips were painted red, and her hair was greased and flattened. She stared towards us at chest height and chewed, like a cow munching its cud.

'I'd like to trade these in for cash,' said May. She nudged me, and I slipped the coins beneath the transparent screen that separated us from the clerk. The clerk glanced at the coins without interest, then handed them to a man at a desk behind her.

'Please fill in this form,' she said, and slipped a piece of paper beneath the screen. May began to write on it. The clerk stared at the top of May's head and continued chewing. The man at the other desk examined the coins through a microscope, weighed them, wrote something on a piece of paper, and handed it to the clerk. All the time she chewed. May slipped her piece of paper back, and the clerk counted out some notes.

'Have a nice day,' she said.

Outside, the clouds had conjoined. The sky was a heavy mass of grey. Even as we stood between the pillars, hesitating, it began to rain in earnest.

'We gotta go down the road to pay the rent now,' said May. 'You'll get to meet our landlord. Real nice guy.'

She drew her coat closer about her and dashed down the steps. I followed her. The water splashed around us off the stone steps and off the paving that lined the road. Nowhere could it sink into the earth; it swam across the stones, forming streams, finding no resting place. It was raining harder as we ran, drumming onto the street and bouncing off again. May disappeared into a doorway, and I followed her.

We stood in a dark hall, dripping water. The rain was a faint roar outside.

'Thought you'd like the water,' said May, grinning at me as she tossed it from her hair. 'Being a sailor.'

There was a door off the corridor. The top half of it was of opaque glass, and had lettering printed onto it. May turned and opened it.

The room we entered was tiny and crowded with people. All Africans, they sat silently on a low bench that ran the room's circumference. There was a woman with three small, sullen children. There were old men with hats and shabby trousers. And there was a young couple who looked around nervously at the others. May and I sat down in the only available space and waited. After a few minutes, an inner door was opened, and a plump young African man came in. He was smartly dressed, and the eyes that sparkled above his puffy, well-fed cheeks were childlike and cruel. Frowning, he looked round at the occupants of the room. Then he noticed May and grinned.

'I've come to see Flanagan,' said May.

The young man nodded his head eagerly. 'I'll tell the boss you here,' he said.

He left us for a few moments, then returned to usher us through to an inner chamber. This room was dominated by a large desk, behind which sat an elderly African. He got up when we entered and greeted us, smiling and extending his arms.

'May,' he said, 'good to see you. Makes a change to have such a pretty face in here.' He guided her to a leather-cushioned chair.

'This is Mister Field,' said May. 'He's a friend of the family. John, meet Mister Flanagan.'

Mr Flanagan gripped my hand and, standing close up against me, looked me up and down. His grip was hard and cold, and the gold rings he wore on his fingers dug into my flesh. He looked at me for a moment unsmilingly, then dropped my hand and turned away. I sat down.

'I've been hoping you'd come see me, May,' he said, returning to the other side of the desk, 'before I'd have to go see you.' He smiled again, and there was a flash of gold in his teeth.

'I've got the rent here,' said May, and she counted out some notes, including those I had given her, onto the desk. 'Now we're paid up till the end of next month, and I'd like a receipt.'

'Okay, okay,' said Mr Flanagan, holding his hands up defensively. 'You gotta learn to do business in a more relaxed fashion,

May.' He picked the notes up and began slowly counting them
out himself. 'And how's the family?' he said as he did so. 'Your
mother doing all right, is she?'

May didn't reply. There was a window at the far end of the
room. Beyond it, figures hurried to and fro through the rain. Mr
Flanagan began laboriously writing out the receipt. Once or twice,
he glanced up at May and smiled. When he had finished writing,
he contemplated the receipt for a moment.

'I know you've had problems getting the money together up
till now,' he said, and glanced at me. 'But that's why I said last
time we could come to an arrangement. It's still possible . . .'

'You've got the goddam rent money,' May interrupted him.
She snatched the receipt from his hand, kicked back her chair,
and marched out of the room.

Mr Flanagan was chuckling and rubbing his long, bony chin with
his hand. I got up to follow May.

'Mister,' said Mr Flanagan sharply.

I looked at him.

'I like your taste,' he said with a sly smile.

May was waiting for me through in the corridor.

'He's full of bullshit, that guy,' she said as we went back out
onto the street. 'Thinks he's fucking Al Capone.'

Apart from this excursion, I was abandoned to my own devices.
May, Eldridge and their mother returned to their regular employ-
ments, from which the parade had provided a kind of holiday and
respite. I took to walking the streets. During these tours, I was
struck above all by the decay of the place. Rows of once fine
houses, passably dressed in brown stone, had fallen apart through
neglect. Many of them had boards across the doors and windows.
Plants and grasses had sprouted from the cellars and through the
cracks in the walls, creating shocks of green, miniature jungles,
amidst the tumbling brickwork. My imagination was curiously
caught by that visual juxtaposition of the crumbling masonry and
the strange, bolting vegetation.

The streets were coated with a glutinous black substance. It
grew slightly sticky beneath the feet in the heat. The city was
like a thin crust spread over the earth. I was walking along a
street near the house one morning, when I came upon more

waste land. There too the ground had been broken, and from among the rubble of the buildings that had once stood there grew many grasses and flowers. Stopping for a moment in the street to gaze at the profusion, I became uncomfortably aware of this hard black crust beneath my feet. All at once I was seized by a violent rage, a desire to reach down and tear apart the case-hardened substance on which I was standing. The maddening strength of my impulse called to mind the mental turmoil I had experienced on my last night aboard the ship. It was as though that had been a premonition and this its fulfilment, its physical fulfilment in my anger against the feel of the hard ground and my impulse to claw it open and rub my hands in the bare, moist earth. For several minutes I must have stood there in rigid stillness, containing the most violent motion within.

At other times, my sense of the strangeness of my surroundings took gentler forms. Some afternoons I wandered far from the house – always taking care to note which way I had come – under the hot, bland sun that blossomed in the afternoons. The streets seemed to stretch for ever, and as I walked between the ruined buildings I fancied how they might once have appeared. The houses, as I have said, still carried some of their former elegance. I could picture in my mind a carriage riding down the street, or a young couple out strolling, she perhaps with a parasol to shield her. These sentimental imaginings, too, were set off in part by the verdure that sprouted from the cracked paving and from the casements of the deserted houses, for by half closing my eyes in the dazzling sunlight I could see the street as an avenue adorned with beautiful light green leaves. Returning to the house in the evening, when the light withdrew and pulled space apart, making the reality around me appear more distant, my dreams and imaginings took off to still weirder heights.

Those evenings when Tommy was away and there was no music were very dull. May and her mother were tired when they returned from work. May would read a book while her mother sat gazing into the light that seeped into every corner of the kitchen. It was always in the kitchen that the family sat in the evening, for as the damp mist closed in at sunset, that small room, with its stove, was the only one that had warmth. Eldridge, activated by that nervous energy that was his characteristic, was more diverting. While there was something unnatural and even disturbing in his agitated demeanour, he was always very kind to me. On about my fifth evening in the house, he arrived home from work with the announcement that he was going straight out again to one of the clubs downtown.

'You wanna come too, John?' he asked eagerly. 'You'd really regret it if you didn't. There's a new disco I'm going to check out.'

I felt May look up at me from her book, her eyebrows raised with interest. I agreed.

'You look after Mister Field, now, Eldridge,' May said caustically. 'I'm sure he isn't used to all that rough excitement.'

'Yeah, sure,' said Eldridge. He clicked his fingers and did a little dance on the floor. 'You got some gear to wear, John, something flashy?'

'I'm afraid I only have another pair of breeches like these.'

'I'm not going there with you looking like that. Shit, they wouldn't let us in.'

'That might be as well,' said May quietly.

'Give us a break, sister,' said Eldridge. He slapped me on the back. 'Don't worry, John, I'll fix you up. I've got just what you need – pair of real smooth pants and a button-down shirt. Guess those old boots'll be okay.'

So – truly fixed up, and with many pleadings from Eldridge that I should take great care of his clothes – we set out. Eldridge's trousers were uncomfortably tight around my stomach and crotch, and absurdly short in the leg, but I bore with him for the sake of his humour. They were a lurid purple colour and the shirt black with a motif of tiny silver stars.

There was no moon that night, only the sickly-sweet yellow light of the lamps bathing the street. Eldridge looked grey and ill in that light. We walked down hundred and thirtieth towards the main street, away from the railroad.

'We'll take the subway,' said Eldridge as we turned into the main street.

The night seemed dangerous; it was filled with roarings that shook the ground and flashing lights that were all around you and then gone. Men shouted unexpectedly from doorways. The air crackled with altercation from the groups that stood in the street, their faces frozen grotesquely as we walked past.

'Almost there,' said Eldridge. 'Hell, seems like the whole town's out tonight.'

There was a hole in the road, and we walked down some steps into it, into a world of hellish white light and metal and thunderous machines that gasped and screamed down black holes. I kept close by Eldridge's side as he wove through the thousands of people. They swirled about like particles of mud disturbed in water. A man read a broadsheet. A woman scolded a child. A beggar collapsed drunk to the floor. Each image was snapped and broken. The white light left no shadow. Each discontinuous image pressed close to my eyeballs.

We waited by some tracks in a hall of iron pillars. Suddenly the tracks crackled, and the ground hummed in sympathy. From out of the entrance to the tunnel, like the chariot of Juggernaut, hurtled an enormous machine. It had a single bright lamp on its front, an eye that searched the darkness before it. It stopped and its side opened to receive us. We stepped on, and it began to move again. It was close and noisy in the carriage as it entered the tunnel and picked up speed. The passengers were pressed together, each bead of sweat on their faces picked out minutely by the lights. I closed my eyes and surrendered myself to the nauseating motion.

'Come on,' said Eldridge. 'This is us.' We had stopped. I opened my eyes and looked around, but Eldridge was already out of the side of the vehicle. I scrambled panicking through the crowd after him.

'Big city, man,' he said when we were up on the street. 'Cooool.' He was strutting along quickly, throwing his feet out in front of him like challenges. The tightness of my trousers made it hard for me to keep up with him.

The buildings were so tall that they arched over above our heads, their dark shapes blocking out the stars. At the level of the street they were an inferno of blazing, flashing light.

'Pretty neat, eh?' said Eldridge, eagerly studying my reaction. 'This is downtown. This is *where it is at*. I mean ALIVE!'

I looked around. My nerves felt jagged, as men are said to feel under fire in battle. At any moment I expected a man to leap from the shadows and stick me in the guts with a bayonet. Yes, perhaps I did feel alive.

'I've never seen anything like it,' I replied, a little tamely. 'You bet,' said Eldridge. He gave a kind of whoop and led me down the street. Some quarter of a mile further on there was a large group of people standing beneath a sign, picked out in lamps, that read 'Electric Visions Niteclub Disco'.

'Yo, my man,' shouted Eldridge. The group wheeled round quickly to look at us. One of them, an African with long hair that had been straightened and greased, broke away and came towards us.

'Give me high five,' he yelled.

'Lay it down, brother,' Eldridge shouted back. They slapped hands and laughed.

'This is John Field,' said Eldridge. 'He's shacking up at our place.'

'Cool,' said the other.

We were absorbed into the group and waited to be admitted to the club. There was little conversation. When a member of the group caught another's eye there was an exchange of nods, or a grin was handed like a mask from the one to the other. They were young, and most of them were Africans. A feeling of nervous tension ran through them like a wind. There was much clicking of fingers, and every now and then someone would break away from the group and pace around in a circle. When the doors were opened the group jerked around as one and went inside.

We paid money and were herded across a hallway lit by red lights. Noise crashed over our heads: trumpets that were not trumpets; drums that were not drums; music like the roaring of the underground machines. It originated from the vast interior of the club. I found it impossible to tell the proportions of this room, for the lamps that lit it flashed on and off in succession, illuminating just one part at any moment. There was a great bare floor in the centre, and round the edge of this, raised on a low platform, were tables and chairs.

Our group sat at the tables, while Eldridge went to get some drinks. We sat stiffly, smoking and occasionally jerking our heads around to see who had come into the club. The noise was like a wall, without shape or interruption. It was as remorseless as the grinding of the vehicle in which we had travelled, as remorseless as the flashing of the lamps that broke the room into a thousand pieces. My companions looked stoical, as though willing them-selves to undergo a test of endurance.

'Having a good time?' Eldridge shouted in my ear when he returned with the drinks.

'I've never seen anything like it.'

'You bet,' he said, and slapped me on the back. I don't think he had heard me.

A lot of people were dancing now on the bare floor in the centre. Those at the tables around the edge watched them.

The dancers danced alone, with great freedom. Each fixed his or her gaze above the heads of the others as though they were afraid to share that freedom that activated their bodies with such lonely spasms.

'Yeah, I like to come here to unwind,' Eldridge was saying. 'Relax.' I nodded, and gratefully took a swig of beer.

I timed the evening by the beers that I drank. There was no other measure. The noise never stopped, and was never different. It was removed from time. I looked all round the place, searching out each corner as it was lit up, to see where the noise came from. It was everywhere and nowhere. The bass notes seemed to vibrate inside one, in the very stomach.

I have no idea how long we were in that place, but I drank ten large glasses of beer before we had left. At one point Eldridge got up to dance with a girl. He did an expanded version of the strutting dance he had done in the kitchen with May, the girl looked uninterested, and Eldridge returned to his seat beside me.

I was almost sorry when we left, feeling a kind of pride that I had survived it for so long. Eldridge's companions had drifted away from us during the course of the evening, and we were left alone. Eldridge was in high spirits as we stumbled away. He was telling me about the interview he was to have the following week for the post of Junior Engineer.

'I'll show those bastards,' he said above the roar of the

machines. 'Joe – he's the guy you met down the railroad, remember?'

'Yes.'

'Yeah, well, he says *no way* they gonna give a job like that to a nigger. "Well, fuck you," I says. "Fuck you, man. 'Cause you're gonna be taking orders from me before too long." Five years I've been on that job, two on night-shift. They've gotta give it to me. You play the system, man, and they'll treat you right.'

When we emerged from the hole again, on the main street near hundred and thirtieth, things were quieter. There were fewer people on the street. But my head was spinning from the beer and the violent sensations of the past hours, and it was still spinning when we made it back to the house and I fell down onto my pallet.

My sleep that night, light and fitful, was crowded with dreams and memories. It started, as I wavered on the edge of unconsciousness, with my mind jolted through a succession of violent images: an enormous machine descending on me, grinding the bones of my legs and cracking my precious fingers; a forest of knives and bayonets shooting at me out of the darkness; a man, which became myself, flinging his limbs about in agony beneath a flashing light. Then these and other diverse images coalesced in the single sensation of the machine, within me now, careering up my spine and exploding into a million fragments in my brain.

This went on, it seemed, for hours, until my exhausted soul slipped down to a yet deeper level of sleep. Then there was peace. I was a child again, standing on the edge of the marsh. It is summer, and leaving you to haggle in the stifling heat of the corn exchange, Mother has brought me out to the coast to watch the horsemen race along the beach from Walberswick to Dunwich. Behind me the marsh stretches away for ever. I stand beneath the clear blue sky on a hillock that seems as high as a mountain. Before me is the vast sea and between my toes, sand and tufts of grass. The riders are ready, their white shirts flapping and billowing. Two of them wear footman's livery. The horses' hooves are pounding the sand. I shout out a couple of times for the joy of hearing my voice carried away by the breeze that sweeps off the sea. 'Woooaah!' Mother is pointing down towards the beach, where the race is about to begin. I shout again, my shout is echoed by the starter, and the horses gallop away across the great curve of the bay. Slowly, so slowly, the horses contract in the hazy heat towards distant Dunwich steeple, which rides its wooded hill like the mast of a ship.

I slip away to the marsh by myself. The marsh holds a secretive peace. Flies buzz about my head as I lie, propped on one elbow, on the long grass that I have flattened around me. In the close heat my worries, my sense of myself, almost dribble away into the smelly, brackish water. Almost, but not quite. A thin thread of anxiety pulls me through each moment. I think about moving my arm from underneath me and lying on my back, think about it for a long time, and then, with resignation, I do it. From within the waterways, over the broad, rustling grasses, comes the shrill, instinctive piping of an oyster-catcher. I lie back and let the mosquitoes graze down my chest.

This dream, this vision that the net of sleep had dragged up from the deeps of my memory, stayed with me for days afterwards. I sat at the window of Tommy's room, gazing at the clouds that crossed the sky like ships, and imagined that I could see right out over the roof-tops, over the oceans, to Dunwich beach. It was one afternoon as I was carried away on one of these meditations that Tommy arrived home. I didn't notice him enter the room.

'You, my man, have got the blues.'

I turned around and saw him standing in the doorway.

'I could swear I saw some blues floating right out that window. What's the matter? You thinking about home?' He put down his bag, to which his horn was tied.

'Let me tell you something,' he continued. 'That's a waste. If you're feeling down like that it means you've got something to say. You should be playing some music, not sitting there like you've just ate too many fries. I can see I've gotta get you working on that fiddle again.'

I could have leapt up and hugged him. Instead I said, 'I'm afraid I haven't played at all. To tell you the truth, I wasn't sure that Peewee would be amenable to loaning me his violin again.'

'Hell, that guy's amenable to anything, so long as it comes with a drink.'

I laughed. 'How were your concerts out of town?'

He flopped down on his pallet. '"Concerts" is pitching it a bit high. Bunch of gigs down the coast, them lily-white joints mostly. I hate playing to those hicks.' He laughed. 'No offence, John.' He lay back with his hands behind his head and whistled a tune. 'Say, John?'

'Yes?'

'You want some air? I was gonna go to the barber's – clean some of that country dirt off and check out the action. You know, catch up on what's been going down around here while I've been away.'

'Certainly.'

'Done.'

The barber-shop was on the main street, not far from the bar where Peewee hung out. A red-striped pole stuck out proudly above the entrance. In the large window that faced onto the street there was a sign that read, 'Soap and shave 50 cents. All types of cut available. We'll also shine your shoes. Just ask the man.' The air inside was so thick with tobacco smoke that my eyes started watering copiously, and for a few moments I could see nothing.

'Hey, Jake,' said Tommy. 'Good to see you. Got back from the sticks this afternoon. Found John here got the blues.'

'Yeah,' said a big voice from somewhere at the back, 'he's got it bad.'

The room exploded with laughter. I smiled, wiped my eyes, and looked around. It was a small room, with fifteen African men squashed into it. They were all sitting except one, the barber. Standing beside an old mirror, he gazed impassively around the room while sharpening his blade vigorously on a leather strop. Jake, the only one I recognised, got up from his chair and shook my hand quite formally.

'Good to see you again, Mister Field. I hope you'll join our little gathering here. You haven't brought your fiddle, have you?'

'I'm afraid not.'

'Well, never mind. We gotta get together again real soon and lay down some tunes. Fact, we can talk about that now. I got us a bunch of dates in town while you've been away, Tommy.'

'Oh yeah?'

'Yeah, I got us a week's residency at the Clef Club and I got us a little rent party on the Saturday where they'll pay us a decent fee.'

'Keep talking.'

'Seventy dollars a man up front for the club. And the dance we'll get ten per cent of the money from the door. Here, I got some cards.' Jake handed around a bright purple card, on which was printed:

Fall in line, and watch your step, For there'll be
Lots of Browns with plenty of Pet At

A Social Whist Party
Given by
Lucille & Minnie
149 West 117th Street, Gr. floor, W,
Saturday Evening, May 22nd

Refreshments Just It   Music Won't Quit

There were murmurs of approval around the company as this was read. Jake told us that we would rehearse that night at Tommy's house, and Tommy hopped into the barber's chair for his shave and cut. I chatted with Jake on musical matters, while Tommy extracted from the barber a gruff account of the doings and tribulations of mutual acquaintances.

'I ever tell you about Jake?' Tommy asked me as we stepped out of the barber-shop and along the street to pick up Peewee's violin. 'When he was my age – no, younger than me – he was the star in this city. He could ask bandleaders a hundred dollars a week. Man, that was unheard of. See they was all used to a melodic kind of trumpet-playing in those days, and Jake Little comes along and he plays running horn. It's like he's out there on the edge the whole time – pushing up to those real high notes, then shooting right down again to the bottom.'

I listened with fascination, gazing into the sunlight that streamed between the Africans on the street.

'About three or four years Jake was up there at the top, playing at all the best places and everybody telling him he's the greatest.

Then the whole thing starts to come apart. He was still a kid. He got to drinking too much, and chasing after women. Pretty soon the dates aren't coming in so fast. It's getting so he's gotta go around looking for work. Then he just kinda disappears. By the time I'm coming on the scene, it's like Jake Little is a legend. Guys would be sitting around swapping the shit, and someone would say, "You ever hear that cat Jake Little play trumpet? He was bad." Soon as you hear a guy talked about like that, like he's a legend, you just know he's through. He ain't even in the ball game no more.

'When I first met Jake it was down there on skid row. I was passing this little bar, and I went in to get myself a drink. There was a band playing, but it was so dark in that place that I couldn't see who the musicians were. Then this guy next to me tells me it's Jake Little playing trumpet, and I'm amazed. I guess I'd kinda assumed he was dead. I went up to him after the set, and he was all strung out. He was living in this real bad boarding house round the corner, and his lip was all fucked up. That's what you get if you start at the top. I was just getting my first band together back then, so I asked him to come in on it with me. He stayed with my family for a while, till he got himself straightened out. That was four years ago, and we've been night-and-day buddies ever since. People don't talk about him the way they used to, like he was a legend, but they're paying cash to hear him play. And that's a whole lot better, let me tell you.'

We had reached the bar. Tommy swung open the door and ushered me in. The place was in a state of mid-afternoon stupor. A scattering of drinkers stewed silently in the sunlight that shafted in from the street. We discovered Peewee in his usual seat, gazing yellow-eyed into an empty glass. Some low murmurings between Tommy, Peewee and the barman issued in an arrangement whereby I handed over some money to the latter on the understanding that he would keep Peewee in drink for a few days. We left with the fiddle and bow.

Finding the house empty when we returned, we sat in the kitchen. I immediately set about examining the violin. There was much that needed doing.

It was dirty, the bridge was out of alignment, and it was badly strung. I got to work. Tommy seemed to be in a pensive mood. He smoked some tobacco and watched me silently while I cleaned the violin and tuned the strings. After a few minutes he gave a deep sigh.

'Yeah,' he said, stretching his arms high above his head, 'I wouldn't change this life for no other.' His voice had a note of sadness in it. 'Your pockets might be light, but you're doing what you choose. Just playing the music. I can't stand no one telling me what to do. I'll tell you, those politicians can do what they like, but they aren't gonna stop me playing this music. Hell they wouldn't bother, 'cause they don't reckon I'm important enough. Tell you something else, I've no intention of getting important, 'cause *that's* when your troubles start.'

He nodded his head conclusively and puffed some more smoke. For a few moments he lapsed into silence again, and I continued rubbing a shine into the surface of the violin. Then he spoke again.

'I've never done nothing but play music,' he said. 'Never washed dishes, or run messages, or worked the railroad. All I've done is play my horn. Course, I'm lucky in that I don't have to pay no rent when I'm not working. My family've helped me a whole lot in that regard over the years. If I couldn't live here, I dunno what I'd 've done sometimes. Had to get a regular job most likely.'

He raised his eyebrows, and became absorbed in his own thoughts again. This time, his silence was so prolonged – and I was so engrossed in the violin, savouring the feel of it resting in my hands – that I had almost forgotten he was there.

'Know what I was saying about getting important?' he said suddenly.

I looked at him.

'Well, I guess I was thinking about May.'

I waited for him to continue.

'You know she's involved with this CAU?' he said. 'Well, May's real smart, and I reckon she could go a long way with them. That's great. Only thing that worries me is that it could hurt her.'

'In what way?' I asked.

He looked at me steadily. 'White folks can be mean. Real mean.

Like I said, if you start sticking out from the crowd, they're gonna pick up on you.'

There was a tense pause. Tommy looked agitated, leaning forward across the table and chewing his lower lip. 'Wanna do me a favour?' he said at last.

'Of course,' I replied. 'What?'

'Keep an eye on May. Check she ain't getting into trouble.'

'I don't see how I could help.'

'Sure you could. You know, have words with people. Check she ain't sticking her neck out.'

'But I know nothing about any of this,' I protested.

'You must know how these things work,' he persisted. His final words hung on his lips for a moment, then spilled out. 'Being white.'

I was troubled. But Tommy was looking at me with anxious eyes, and despite my misgivings I could not refuse his obscure request.

'Well, I'll do what I can,' I said. 'But I can promise nothing.'

'I knew you wouldn't let me down,' he said, smiling with relief. 'You just carry on with your fiddle in here. I'll be upstairs playing my horn.' He left.

For a long while I sat turning over in my mind the conversation I had just had with Tommy. It had left me confused, wishing I knew more of what he expected me to do. I was on the point of going upstairs after him to ask him to explain the matter more, when my eye was caught by the violin and bow on the table before me. I could not resist picking them up and playing a few notes.

The bothersome matter of May and the CAU quickly slipped from my attention. As has always happened when I have not played for a long time, an initial facility was succeeded by a painful realisation of the rebuilding work that was needed in the weak passages of my technique. Trills, scales, chords, arpeggios, the *spiccato*, the *tremolo*, the *sautille*, the *ricochet* and the *staccato*; I went through them all till I was at least partially satisfied. And then I tried to imitate the music that I had heard Peewee play. I was able to recall some of the lines, but they seemed tortuous and jerky beneath my fingers. I worked harder at them, straining to remember exactly how they had sounded when Peewee had

played them. Try as I might, there was something there, something strange and beyond my previous experience, that I could
not capture. But the endeavour absorbed me; I must have played
for hours, because when I next glanced at the small kitchen
window it was dark. I stopped playing and took the violin from
beneath my chin, exhausted.

'That's pretty good.' May was leaning against the doorway,
her dark face obscured by shadow.

'How long have you been there?' I asked.

She moved forward into the light. 'Oh, long enough.'

'Not too long, I hope?'

'Afraid not, Mister Field,' she said, smiling. 'Only just got back
from work.' She sat down – her legs apart, her elbows leaning
on her knees – and rested her head in her hands. 'God, I'm beat,'
she said, to the floor.

I put the violin down on the table. My hard work had filled me
with confidence and well-being. I looked down at May. She looked
collapsed and exhausted, and her air of vulnerability brought back
to mind my conversation with Tommy. My new-found sense of
power made his commission seem less daunting. I saw a plan of
action.

'May?' I said.

'Mmmmhhmm?'

'Do you think it might be possible for me to come to one of the
meetings of the Civil Advancement Union? As a foreigner, you
see, I'm fascinated by the affairs of state here.'

'Sure,' she murmured without raising her head. 'I'll take you
along.'

'Many thanks. I shall look forward to it.'

From the end of the corridor I heard a door bang, then Jake's
voice shouting up the stairs to Tommy.

'I'll have to go now,' I said. 'The other musicians are arriving.'

'Yeah,' she said. 'Yeah, you go along now.' She bowed her
head again to the floor.

The musicians were crowding through the entrance into the
corridor. In addition to Jake, there were the three I had met on
my first day in the city – the guitarist, the tall bass-fiddle player,
and the fat one with his drums. The last I helped with his

equipment up the dark, narrow stairs – carefully protecting the precious violin in the crook of my arm. Once in the cramped confines of Tommy's room, we kicked aside the pallets on which Tommy and I slept, and set ourselves up so that we would be playing to the black shiny eye of the window. Jake and Tommy huddled together and adjusted the pitch of their instruments till they were in accord. Then the three string players – Dan, the bass fiddler and myself – tuned ourselves with them, while the drummer banged annoyingly behind us. I did the best I could in all of this without knowing what pitches I was tuning with, then waited to see what would happen.

'Right,' said Jake cheerfully, 'let's kick off with the Sidewalk Blues. You just join in when you feel comfortable, Mister Field.'

The guitarist began by himself with stomping chords, interrupted by a thump from the drums. Jake took up the rhythm with a flowing figure that lasted but a couple of measures, before it too was stopped by a thump. The figure was passed, as though never broken, to Tommy; who played with it, twisted it a little, and handed it back again. Jake's reply was punctuated again by the rhythm section, and as if angered by these interruptions he set out on a low, snarling melody. The others pushed him on with chords placed at the back of each measure. This syncopation had the curious effect of flipping the tune upside down – exposing, so to speak, its underbelly. Jake rose through the registers to a twirling fanfare.

There began a smooth, almost mournful, chorale over a marching bass line. From the start I had been eager to join in, but had felt too bewildered and bewitched to insert myself into the shifting currents of the music. But as the chorale began, the fingers of my left hand began instinctively to feel over the strings for the harmonies. I, too, began to play.

The beautiful figure that Tommy, Jake and I played in harmony was repeated over and over again, as though the march were marching off into a dream. There was a lovely flexibility to the phrase; it began with long tones that swelled and closed, then finished with a dozen dancing notes that tripped over each other in their haste to attain a resolution. Jake dropped out. Now the sound was softer edged; I could hear now how well I blended with Tommy's horn. I looked at the guitarist. His eyes were closed, in a kind of rapture, but when I looked at him he seemed to nod his head as if in approval. Pride and confidence flowed through me to the tips of my fingers. I warmed my tone still more, adding my own embellishments. Even better, I had the sense to stop and listen when the harmonies suddenly changed, and Jake came screaming in against a heavier beat. He played like a man possessed, hurling phrases down like thunderbolts, so hard that they bounced off the bottom of his range and came shooting up again. Tommy joined in, and when Jake was going down, Tommy would be coming up. All was glorious confusion.

When the piece ended, with a great roll on the drums and cymbal crash, the room was hot and close. There were beads of moisture on the black glass eye before us. Tommy opened the casement, and the cool night air blew in.

'"Save It, Pretty Mama",' said Jake. He clicked his fingers to indicate the slow, restful tempo. The guitarist played an introduction, and as he did so Jake raised his trumpet slowly and wearily, as though lifting a burden, to begin his tale. He told it with a humble resignation that became a kind of humour. Rising in the scale, he strained for the notes with a growl that signified pain; descending, the notes slid down into place as though under the force of God or Fate's ordination that it ever should be thus. Leaning his head to the side, he told his tale out of the open window, over the same roof-tops where I had sent my dreams and memories. But my meditations had dissipated in the bland, all-seeing daylight; it was night now, and the darkness closed in around the single shining sound of Jake's story. As he finished, he turned to me and raised his eyebrows. Without hesitation, I took up my fiddle and replied in kind.

Were it not for the yellow light that reached up and scraped the night sky, Father, I could have been back in the attic room in Clerkenwell to which I fled from home. There, when my day had finished with the sweeping and scrubbing of the physician's rooms downstairs, I would play my violin by the open window. Shouting and drunken singing would rise like a swelling tide from the street below. With every particle of my child's body I willed my music to escape the sweet smell of shit from the gutters, and disappear up to the stars. There were no yellow lights there, just a deep blackness receding through the brick maze of London's streets. For me – freed from the bonds that had held me; freed from childhood, which is never one's own – the darkness was a void which I needs had to fill with my newly stirring sense of myself. Your memory, I confess, was like that of a cage to a song-bird that has escaped its prison. The very order of your existence – the regularity of its pattern, the ruled lines in your ledger books – appeared to me as the bars of a prison which I had left behind me. Now, of course, my perspective is changed. I have seen other bars rise up around me, from which I sought to escape and free myself. I have come to see them, in part, as the constructs of my own restless spirit.

Did I but know it, another set of bars was about to press up around me. For it was a few days later that I went to the meeting of the CAU with May. My misgivings and confusions about Tommy's request had been supplanted in these intervening days by a strong desire for adventure, a yearning to play an active part in some public affair of the city. Hitherto I had let myself be carried along by events too much. As I considered the matter, I found myself thinking back to Sergei's singleminded pursuit of the orcas. This episode became in my mind a model, in its psychological aspects, for my new wilfulness; but whereas Sergei's object was the destruction of whales, mine was the protection of May against the intrigues and cabals of politics.

What precisely I would do to discover the obscure forces ranged against May, I had no idea. I went to the meeting trusting to my intuitive sense to seize the opportunity of the moment. We arrived rather late at the church hall where it was being held, and I slipped into a seat at the back while May took her place on the platform. An impassioned speech was in progress, bursting with biblical references and invocations to the audience's collective hopes and dreams. The man's voice was musical, with litanies rolling off his tongue in great waves. The Africans in the audience were moving restlessly, swaying like corn before a wind. Now and then someone would moan and cry out in agreement with the speaker. For a few moments I succumbed to the emotion about me. But then I remembered why I had come, and steeled myself against any distraction, any deviation from the path I was fixed upon. Looking around me to examine the company, I quickly spotted the only face that I knew, that of the tall white gentleman I had met at the parade.

At once a plan of campaign sprung to mind. Mr S—— was both a member of the CAU and white. If I could befriend him and gain his confidence, I might be able to draw from him some information on the workings of the organisation and its opponents. Satisfied with this tactical manoeuvre, I sat back and awaited my moment. At the end of the speech, which was loudly applauded, it was announced that there would be a short interval. As the members of the audience stood up and began talking excitedly among themselves, I hurried over to Mr S—— and introduced myself.

'Good to see you again, Mister Field,' he said. 'Yeah, I remember you from the parade. What's new?'

I had not liked the man when I had first met him, and I liked him no more now. There was something in the way that he smiled down at me that I found offensive. He was much taller than I, and I deliberately spoke quietly so that he had to stoop to hear me.

'I'd like to know you, sir,' I said. 'I have a great interest in the workings of the CAU, and I believe you, as one of its luminaries, could enlighten me.'

This had a pleasing effect. He looked me up and down with interest.

'Well, I'm always ready to help out someone with a genuine concern. Perhaps you'd like to fill me in on your own background. You're from . . . ah . . . England, I believe?'

I told him my story, how I had come ashore and been taken up by Tommy's family, and how I was now playing with Tommy's band.

When I had finished, he coughed, pushed his spectacles up his nose, and, with a nervous chuckle, said: 'Well, your case is certainly, ah, a little unusual, Mister Field.'

He leant towards me confidentially.

'Do you mean to say that you're, ah, *living* with May's family, that is, in their house?'

'Yes.'

He raised his eyebrows, a smile pinned to his large mouth. I was uncomfortably aware that we were the only white people in the hall, and that we were conspicuously huddled together apart from the others. As Mr S—— spoke, I looked past him, trying to catch sight of May.

'And playing this music – you intend to make that your career, do you?' he continued.

'I have not really considered the matter,' I said. 'I do not have any fixed plans.' I was finding this inquisition a little unsettling. Indeed, it was not at all what I had in mind when I had entered into the conversation. Now I too laughed nervously, and added: 'It's an adventure, I suppose.'

'Ah, I see,' said Mr S——, and he smiled down at me even more benignly, 'An adventure. You know, it might be good to regularise your position here. Don't want people thinking you're totally off the wall.' He left a pause for this to sink in, then went on: 'Always good to get some order into your life, I say. You know, figure out where you're at and where you're going.'

'Yes,' I said absently. May had caught my eye. She was still up on the platform, talking with a group of Africans.

'Perhaps that's what you're really looking for, to get some order into your life?'

'Oh, certainly.'

'Now we're getting some place,' he said, rubbing his hands. 'I think I might be able to help you, Mister Field. I've always been ready to help out an immigrant who arrives in town not knowing how things operate.' He put his hand on my shoulder. 'I may be able to get you a job in our office downtown.'

I looked at him in amazement, and was on the point of speaking, when he interrupted: 'Now hold your horses. I can't promise anything. I'll have to talk to some people and get back to you on this one. But I think we just might be able to work something out. What do you say?'

I thought quickly. Perhaps this was just the opportunity I had been waiting for.

'You're most obliging,' I said, carefully.

'Great.' He looked over his shoulder into the body of the hall,

where the audience was taking its seats again. 'I'll drop you a line
at May's place soon. Let you know what's cooking.' He gave me
a wink. 'Enjoy the rest of the meeting.'

After the meeting, I walked back to the house with May. She
said nothing about Mr S——.

There was much else to think about over the next few days,
for the performances at the Clef Club were approaching, and
we were rehearsing every afternoon to perfect that complex
alternation of solo and *tutti* episodes that was the hallmark of our
orchestra. My role was primarily to add a richness of colour to
the *tutti*, though as my confidence grew, and I began to master
the kind of figurations and embellishments that Jake and Tommy
used, I was allowed to have some solos myself. In particular,
Jake made an arrangement of 'La Follia', in which I played the
melody while Tommy wove an *obbligato* part around me. Every
morning I rose early and practised these solos by myself for a
couple of hours, then went out walking and ran through them
again in my head, thinking of new variations.

It was summer now, and a peculiar damp heat had descended
on the city. In the mornings, the black-crusted streets glistened
with traces of moisture from the warm fog that had shrouded
them during the night. The strong, hot sun forced its way through
the haze as the day progressed, till by afternoon it had lifted the
moisture and was beginning to bake the city. I walked past the
ruined houses that were by now almost familiar to me. The music
I had learnt flowed through me. In the sticky furnace of the
summer, the plants and grasses that grew through the crumbling
masonry were shooting up and turning to a richer green. Humming
all the while, I would look deep into the leaves, sometimes
stopping to peer down a deserted alley where a sapling had forced
a passage up through a wall into the sunlight. There occurred
to me a connection between the music and this illicit foliage,
as though each note were a vibrant green leaf and the whole
music some strange blue fruit that had been shockingly borne
on the brittle boughs of the city. I hunted the thought, through
forgotten alleys past deserted houses, but it eluded me like a
melody that twists and turns on for ever and never reaches a
cadence.

In the evenings, after I had finished working with the band, I sometimes went drinking with Tommy to the bar where Peewee sat like a forlorn monument, or I walked down to the railroad with May. There was a distance now between May and me, for as we sat on the bank by the small park looking down at the tracks that disappeared into the misty night, and she talked of the CAU and all the hope of a new life that it held for her, my thoughts were drawn to the tall white figure of Mr S——. I grew to loathe the memory of his smooth forehead caressing the air as he stooped to hear me. But this dislike served merely to focus my mind infuriatingly on what he had said and the sly derision that lay behind his smile. His words were beginning to acquire the status of a challenge, an insidious sneer at everything I had valued. I could not voice this to May, so instead I interrogated her about the CAU to discover if Tommy's fears were founded in fact. But my heart was no longer in this, for I could only think about the CAU in connection with Mr S—— and with Mr S—— in connection with my 'irregularity' and 'lack of purpose'. The promise I had made to Tommy had well nigh disappeared from my mind. I came to regret that it was only on account of this promise that I had made contact with Mr S—— at all.

On the day of our first performance at the Clef Club, we practised there in the afternoon. It was a large room with a bar in one corner and a low ceiling of wooden rafters. The chairs were stacked up on the small round tables, and a boy was mopping the floor around them. Jake had written out in order all the tunes we were to play that night. They came in two halves, and all the pieces in which I played were in the second half. This was to be the programme for all five nights we were to play at the Clef Club. We played through a few of the numbers, and Jake said they sounded all right and that we should all go home and get some rest and be back sharp at ten o'clock. To me the music had sounded lost in the empty hall, and I had had to strain to fill it with the sound of the violin. I said as much to Tommy as we walked back home.

'Don't worry about that,' he said. 'You get a bunch of people in there, soak up the sound, and it's completely different. Tell you, you got an audience in front of you, especially like the crowd

you get in that Clef Club, and you're talking a whole different
scene as far as playing music's concerned, 'cause that's when
things start getting *hot*. The crowd that go down there, they
know their music. I mean they dig it, but they *know* it.' He looked
at me and laughed.

We spent the next few hours sitting on our pallets in Tommy's
room smoking tobacco. They dragged past very slowly. Tommy
cleaned his horn meticulously with an old rag, till it blazed in the
sunlight that streamed through the haze of blue-grey smoke. I
checked my strings and rubbed down Peewee's old violin. But
this did not take long, and when I had finished there was nothing
to do but gaze out of the window and feel the nervousness and
anticipation churning in my guts. The evening gradually darkened
the street. The door downstairs banged as first May and then
her mother came in from work. Tommy was fiddling with some
fine adjustments to the keys of his horn. Every now and then he
would pick it up and play a flurry of notes. At one point, May put
her head round the door and asked us if we wanted some dinner.
Tommy shook his head without looking up from his horn. I said
I didn't really feel like eating. May wished us luck and said she'd
be along to hear us the following night. Then the lamps in the
street came on and flooded the room with yellow light. I leaned
back against the wall and waited. The excitement of the day
seemed to have drained my body of its strength. The room was
warm from all the sunshine that had streamed in through the
window. I began thinking about previous times I had felt like this,
in anticipation of concerts I had played with Monsieur Yepanchin
in London. I began to fall asleep.

'Well, I guess we'd better get moving.' Tommy woke me.

The Clef Club was draped around its wide doorway with a
striped canvas awning. From this there fluttered a banner that
read, 'MIDNITE SHOW JAKE LITTLE & HIS ORCHESTRA
RESERVED SEATS ON SALE NOW'. A crowd of Africans and
Europeans milled around the entrance. The light from the yawning
doors outshone the dull orange glow in the street. We marched
straight through the crowd into the club, swinging our instruments
importantly by our sides. Inside, a woman was singing to an
already full house, accompanied only on the keyboard. The room

was dark and secret, and she was picked out on the low stage by a single bright light. Her pure, light voice swam through rippling chords as though through water. The audience was quiet and attentive, apart from an obstinate hum of conversation from around the bar. The singer leant one hand lightly on the long body of the keyboard, swaying in slow circles to the rhythm of the song.

> *I heard a woman on her own*
> *Talkin' on the telephone*
> *To a lovin' man who's been away*
> *From her just a week today.*
> *She said, 'You'd better hurry home*
> *'Cause your mama's all alone.*
> *Got to have some lovin' daddy here,*
> *Let me whisper in your ear:*
>
> *Papa if you want it*
> *You'd better come and get it*
> *'Cause I'm savin' it all for you.*
> *If you do, sweet papa,*
> *You surely won't regret it –*
> *I love you truly, 'deed I do.*
>
> *Sweet mama's got*
> *What you need.*
> *It ain't a lot,*
> *But always guaranteed.*
> *Papa if you want it*
> *You'd better come and get it*
> *'Cause I'm savin' it all for you.*
>
> *Papa if you want it*
> *You'd better come and get it*
> *'Cause I'm savin' it all for you.*
> *If you do, sweet papa,*
> *You surely won't regret it –*
> *I love you truly, 'deed I do.*

To love me, hon' –
Quite all right.
I'm all alone,
I've nothin' on tonight.
Good daddy, roll
What I've got.
It might get cold,
So get it while it's hot.
Papa if you want it
You'd better come and get it
'Cause I'm savin' it all for you.'

Jake, it transpired, was the source of the unwanted accompaniment from the back. He sat perched on a high stool at the bar surrounded by musicians, those in our band and some others I had seen with him and with Tommy. They were bunched together in a close and exclusive group. The talk was passed slowly about between them, licked into shape every now and then by Jake's laconic, unhurried laugh.

'Here they are, the terrible twins,' he boomed out when he saw us. Behind us, the woman's voice floated softly on. 'You all right, John? You look scared shitless. Like you've seen a ghost.' His interlocutors turned round and laughed for a moment.

'Rather nervous, perhaps,' I replied.

'These men need some liquor,' cried Jake, and he hailed the barman in a fit of mock panic. We sat down, and the men resumed their talk.

'He must have been about the hottest man on the instrument in town around that time.'

'You kidding? He was playing everywhere.'

'Yeah, till Davis blew him off the stand that night.'

'Yeah, that's when he learnt about jam sessions.'

'Didn't see him around too much after that.'

'He was nowhere.'

My attention shifted back and forth between the tight circle of conversation and the life of the club outside it. I looked out over the array of heads at the singer. She had her eyes fixed almost defiantly above the audience at the back of the room. Her

accompanist, a serious young African, glanced up at her occasionally from the keyboard as though searching her for some sign.
The song ended, and the audience clapped. Jake and the others
stopped their conversation, clapped too (one of them put two
fingers in his mouth and whistled), then took up where they had
left off.

'Shit, that was a hell of an evening. That cop knocked him
so hard one of his teeth fell out in the middle of the gig next
night.'

'Sure thing. I remember – I was there.'

The woman sang her last song, bowed to the audience, and
nodded smiling to the young man at the keyboard. A roar of
conversation burst in the crowd, filling the space that she had
held by herself. They surged around us at the bar.

'Well, this is us,' said Jake, heaving himself off the stool.

'Yeah, here goes nothing,' laughed Tommy.

I stayed by the bar while the others set up on the stage. They
opened with 'Doctor Jazz':

> *Hello, Central, give me Doctor Jazz*
> *He's got what I need I say he has.*

Jake's great black voice rolled down the room between the tables.
From the instrumental introduction, a proud fanfare that shot like
a rocket up to the rafters, the drinkers around me had stopped
talking and turned to watch the performance. As he sang, Jake's
arms and legs twitched in rhythm with a peculiar joyful excitement.
The gestures were wild and exaggerated, like those of a puppet.
But, watching the broad-chested figure that filled the stage, one
was continually aware, through the smoke and dim light, of its
humanity. He transcended his role. My attention drifted back and
forth between the puppet and the person; the figure up on the
stage seemed to stand at the hinge between the two, neither
human nor more or less than human. This slow rhythm of my
changing perception throbbed against the beat of the music as the
band moved straight into the next number. I looked down to my
right at a young white man, like myself. He sat slumped forward
in his chair and gazed with a beatific smile at the floor. His head

nodded and shook to a slow beat somewhere beyond the music.
Everything seemed to be moving very slowly. Shocks of sound,
like slow explosions, burst from Jake's golden trumpet. I began
to walk down between the tables. I felt my arms swinging loose
at my sides and the music driving up against me. For a few long
moments I would feel that I had reached home, a place where I
could be happy and safe and could flourish, where my hopes and
aspirations could shape a physical reality through the strings
beneath my fingers and the waves of music in the air. Then in a
cascade of drums and a roar of noise from the audience crashed
down on me the awareness that this was real and true. The wave
swept on past and lifted me again. Tommy's horn snaked around
my legs and drew me forward till I was standing right in front of
the stage, looking up at them. They looked larger beneath the
bright lights. They were gathering up all the life in the room,
sucking it in, and hurling it out again, transfigured, beneath the
low rafters. A hundred hands crashed together behind me.

'Yeah,' said Jake. 'Gonna take five now and be back with another
set.' He glanced down at me. 'And here's the new member of the
Jake Little Orchestra all ready to give you some fancy fiddle work
when he gets back. So stick around, folks. Thank you.'

There was some laughter and shouting from the audience.
A rush of self-consciousness nerved me, pulling me from the
dream-like state into which I had fallen. I climbed up onto the
stage to congratulate Jake and Tommy.

'Yeah,' said Tommy, 'it's going okay. I'll get us all a taste from
the bar.' He jumped down from the stage and made his way
through the crowd.

'You all ready to play?' asked Jake.

'Yes,' I said firmly.

'That's good,' he said. 'You come on over and sit with me a
minute. I wanna have a few words with you before we go on
again.'

We sat down on two chairs at the back of the stage, and I
watched as Jake carefully wiped the sweat from his face with a
white cloth. When he had finished, he smiled at me.

'Well, I think you're gonna do all right tonight,' he began.
'You're playing pretty good now. Yeah, beginning to get the hang

of it. There's just one thing you ain't quite got.' He paused, and shook his head. 'It's got something to do with what we was talking about that time we first met, about me coming from the islands and shit. It was something I picked up from my people there, that they'd brought with them in their time. It was in the way they talked, the way they made music. The way they did everything. See, it never does to say anything direct. You gotta skirt around it or lead up to it or something. *Make* something of it. You telling a story, you don't just jump straight to the end and say "Well, the man died", or "Yeah, he got the girl", 'cause if you do that it ain't a story. No, you lead up to it, you wind around a while till you eventually fetch up at that point. Same way, if you playing a note on your fiddle, the people out there gotta understand *why* you're playing that note. You don't just play it, you *explain* it to them. Sure, sometimes you play around with them, like sometimes you'll be playing some lick that's as old as the hills and everybody knows it, and then right at the end you'll slip in something different, to surprise them. That's the kinda thing that keeps them listening. Mind you, you start doing that all the time like some of these young guys you hear, you're gonna start losing contact with the audience. Then it ain't music. Dunno what it is, but it ain't music. Anyway, what I'm getting at so far as you're concerned is that every note has to be a story, coming from somewhere, going some place else, so you don't wanna be scared of sliding into the note or just kinda *easing* your way out of it again. Sometimes, you know, you can go and just suggest a whole bunch of notes, not really play them out, and the people out there'll pick up on what your getting at. They'll pick up on it. You see?'

'I think so.'

Tommy came up to us with some drinks.

'What's up?' he asked Tommy.

'Oh, just going over some basics.'

Tommy laughed. 'Yeah, those basics.'

Jake looked at him affectionately. 'Tommy reckons he's heard it all before.' He took the beer from him. 'I was just telling John here to loosen up a bit when he's playing.'

'He's loose, man. Told me he was – what was it? – yeah, I remember, told me he was an errant traveller.'

'An errant what?' said Jake.

'A traveller, man. An errant traveller.'

'Oh yeah.'

The second set kicked off with a quick blues. Jake had asked
me to take the breakout and first solo. The moment came, the
drummer launched me with a thunderous roll, and I was left flying
in empty space for a few moments, before the band crashed back
in behind me. Of the experience of playing that night I can
remember little, for such was the intensity, the concentration,
that there was no room for reflection, or for any feeling other
than a churning excitement. Monsieur Yepanchin had taught me
as a child how to improve upon a ground bass and execute the
divisions of a tune. I drew upon that teaching now, with trills,
arpeggi, acciaccature, gruppetti, appoggiature and all the other
devices in my armoury. When Tommy and Jake were playing
their solos, I would move to the back of the stage and quietly
test some embellishments, then move forward when it came my
turn to prove myself before the audience. So that while I was
prominent only occasionally, I was playing without cease, a stream
of sweet sound that I could feel as solidly as the strings beneath
my fingers.

We played 'La Follia'. Jake had composed a beautiful arrangement for it that grew through six variations to a noble and tragic
climax. We ended the performance with 'Fidgety Feet', which
was lightning quick, the *ostinato* figure chasing itself wildly around
the room. I remember Jake thrusting the bell of his trumpet to
every corner of the place, as though testing the walls' capacity
to hold him.

When the show had finished, when the last customer had left
and we had packed away the instruments, we drifted out into the
warm, damp night. We stood outside the club in the night mist,
chatting and enjoying our exhausted indecision. The guitarist led
us to a small bar he knew a few yards along the road, where we
drank and talked about the music. When Tommy and I finally got
home, I took a last look out the window of his room and saw dawn
breaking over the roof-tops.

Ever since I came to the age of self-awareness, Father, and
began to look in upon my own life, I have dreamt of a place where

I might be happy. Indeed, knowing how you hate a romantic and love to see him suffer, I could get my satisfaction of you now by ending my account here. But as the poet says: 'Enjoy the bright, keep it turned up perpetually if you can, but be honest, and don't deny the black.' So I will on, and tell you how I received a letter from Mr S——.

It was the next day, after we had played our second performance at the Clef Club. I rose late and, leaving Tommy to his slumbers, went down to the kitchen. I found May sitting at the table, and on the table was a white envelope.

'This came for you.' She handed me the letter and looked down at the table. I read it.

S—— Communications Inc.,
114 W 10th St 257
Dear Mr Field,
    Further to our conversation of the 19th, would you come to my office at 11.00 AM on the 27th. We can discuss then your position and prospects.
Best wishes,
Yours sincerely,

Mike S——

'You're really settling in now, aren't you, Mister Field?' said May. She was still gazing down at the table. 'Getting mail and all now.' The silence she left behind her was tense and inquisitorial.

'Yes,' I said hesitantly. 'It's from Mr S——.'

She was silent for a moment, nodding her head and smiling. Then she said quietly, 'Yeah.'

For a few moments longer she looked down at the table, then, pulling herself out of the mood that had gripped her, she looked up at me with a more open smile on her face.

'Hell,' she said, 'there's no reason why you should be any different.'

'Different from what?' I said.

Her smile faded. She shook her head and sighed.

'Look, forget I said anything,' she said. 'Please, just forget it.
I've gotta go to the store.' She got up and left the room.

I put the letter down on the table, sat in the chair that May
had vacated, and looked long and hard at the piece of paper before
me. The front door banged, and a draught from the corridor lifted
the letter from the wooden table top. I pressed my hand down
on it to keep it in place, then released it again when the gust of
air had passed. The morning was bright outside. The kitchen's
small casement was open, and sunlight seeped onto the table.
The paper was dazzling white, large, with a few lines of black
print spread across it.

Your position and prospects . . . I half-closed my eyes. The individual letters and words coalesced in unbroken black traces across
the whiteness of the page, like smears left in the track of an insect.
I pulled them back into focus. They were like a challenge lying,
unanswered, on the table before me. The few words seemed to call
everything into question. *Position and prospects*. They were almost
the kind of words you might have spoken. Now that I came to think
of it, it struck me forcibly that I had little of either. Seen in this harsh
light, the events of my recent past – my decision to leave the ship;
being taken up by Tommy's family; playing in the band – they all
seemed chaotic, disorderly, even somewhat disreputable. *Take
control of affairs*, the piece of paper before me seemed to say. *Do
this*. The music in the Clef Club – for a few moments that seemed
transitory and insubstantial.

I was able to postpone the decision as to whether to obey Mr
S——'s summons for some days, as there was much music to be
played. But there was one incident that served to remind me
painfully of the matter. It was the evening of the following
day, when Tommy and I were preparing for our penultimate
performance at the Clef Club. We were in the kitchen, where we
had been hard at work all afternoon, composing and coordinating
some new melodies and sequences of chords. Tommy's mother
had come in wearily from her employment and begged us to carry
on playing while she rested in her usual chair. She was singing
quietly along with us, Tommy's horn dancing around her, when
the front door slammed, and Eldridge came charging down the
corridor into the kitchen.

'Hey, you guys,' he exclaimed, waving a piece of paper at us, 'I got some great news. You ready for it?'

We nodded.

'I got myself an interview for the job. No kidding: here it is, in black and white.'

'Pretty damn good, huh?' said Eldridge.

Tommy handed me the piece of paper, and I read it:

Dear Sir,
Junior Engineer, Uptown-Suburban Section
Please be ready to attend an interview for the above post at Head Office on the 27th of this month. You will be notified in due course as to the exact time of your appointment.
Yours sincerely,

P. D. Walsh, Personnel Manager

'Twenty-seventh,' he continued. 'That's next Thursday. By next Friday you'll be looking at a Junior Engineer.'

'Well, I'm very proud of you, Eldridge,' said his mother. 'Only don't raise your hopes too high now, will you? There's sure to be a whole lot of other guys going for the job well as you.

'Don't worry, Ma,' said Eldridge, taking the piece of paper back from me. 'I've got everything under control.'

Tommy gave his brother a smile and a nod, then picked up his horn again and began polishing it.

May came with Tommy and me to the Clef Club that night. She sat at a table at the front to hear us perform. Tommy played up to her presence, winking at her, and once, during a slow ballad, getting down on his knees and playing right to her. May thought this very amusing, though she waved him away in mock annoyance. The more she waved him away, the further he leant out towards her and the more fervently he pleaded to her with his horn. The rest of the audience, observing this touching scene, hummed with laughter. Soon after the beginning of the second set, when I had joined the others on the stage, a handsome young African came up to May's table and sat drinking with her for the rest of the show. I found myself distracted by pangs of absurd jealousy. Every now and then, as I played, I would glance down to the table to see May talking freely and happily with the man.

'Weren't your best night,' Jake said to me quietly as we packed up the instruments at the end of the show.

'No, it wasn't,' I said. 'My apologies.'

'Hell, don't apologise,' he said. 'Happens to us all some nights.' He put his hand on mine. 'You're all right.'

By the time Tommy and I came off the stage, May's gallant had drifted off into the departing crowd. She was sitting alone at the table.

'Hey, you guys are good,' she said, getting up from her chair as we approached. 'Even you, Mister Field.' She laughed. 'You're all pretty hot.'

For a few moments the three of us stood awkwardly around the table. I gazed down at my boots, suddenly feeling rather miserable. Tommy also had his head downcast, and May was looking at us, from the one to the other.

'Well, what's with you two? Somebody just die?' There was no reply. 'What do you say we all go for a walk someplace. Go on, Tommy, you go and get a bottle from the bar there, and we'll go off somewhere and drink it, the three of us.'

Tommy bought a bottle of spirit from the bar, and we walked down to the railroad. It was a clear night, colder than it had been. The darkness was almost solid, like the flanks of a wild animal. We could hear the train whistles shrieking somewhere out there in the darkness. We drank.

'So Eldridge'll be running this lot before too long,' said May. The rumble of wheels on the metal tracks created a distant turbulence.

'Yeah,' said Tommy slowly, and he took another swig of the spirit. 'Maybe. Though if you want my opinion, I doubt whether they'd give a nigger a job like that. He'd be a white man's boss. Can't have that.'

'You don't know that for sure. He's got the experience, he's good at the work. He could get it.'

'Well, how come he's been doing that job all these years? How come he's got so much experience? 'Cause they're never gonna give him promotion, that's why.'

'Well, what else is he gonna do? He can't play the music. You're lucky, you know that, brother? What else he gonna do? Lie back and let the world pass him by? Listen, Tommy, you've got no right calling him a white man's nigger or an Uncle Tom, just 'cause he takes orders from white men. What else he gonna do? You tell me that.'

'Well, that's his question. You should be asking him.'

'Yeah, and he's found the answer. I respect him for that.'

'Found their answer, more like,' said Tommy in a low, almost angry, voice. 'Taken the hook. All that talk of "I'm getting ahead and fuck the rest."'

'Sure, he plays the game by their rules. But he's got no other game. No choice, least not yet.'

'He'll end up like Flanagan,' Tommy shouted. 'A white man's nigger with a big car and a wallet full of other men's money.'

'Well, at least he brings home some cash,' said May fiercely. 'And anyway, you play for white audiences when you can get the work.' She stood up. 'I'm going. 'Night, John.'

After she had gone we were silent for a long time, passing the bottle back and forth. I was turning what Tommy had said over and over in my mind. Eventually, I broke the silence.

'I'm a white man,' I said.

For a moment he was quiet. Then he threw himself back on the grassy bank and laughed long and hard up into the night sky. He turned to me with his eyes still sparkling.

'No you ain't,' he said.

The next night, Father, we played our final show at the Clef Club. Favourable reports of our playing had circulated, and for this, our last appearance, there was a long queue at the door. Worried by my poor performance the previous night, and also to escape the tensions that were coming to the fore in Tommy's family, I spent most of the day playing my violin out in the little park above the railroad tracks. It was good to play out in the sunlight, the sound close and dead in the open air. I was reminded of the times when, as a boy, I would take my violin down to the Cam and play on the river bank, until evening closed in and the insects began to bite. My solitary practice by the railroad may have done some good, for I played much better that night. The whole band was lifted by the excitement of the occasion and by the large, enthusiastic audience.

At the end of the performance we had to rush straight out to the rent party at which we were to play. We had some difficulty finding the address we had been given on the printed card. The warm night mists had closed in again, and we wandered lost for some time along the streets of collapsed houses. We located the party in the end by the noise that burst from the open windows – laughter, shouting, singing, and a piano playing in an upstairs room. Great piles of rubbish, rank with decay, blocked the street outside. With difficulty we climbed over them with our instruments. I carried my violin in one hand and a drum in the other, only to discover a large gentleman standing in the doorway.

'Anything I can do for you?' he demanded.

'Yeah,' said Jake, 'I'm Jake Little, and this is my band. We're playing here tonight.'

'You're late,' the man said, stepping aside. 'Go set up out back there. I'll tell Lucille you're here.'

We struggled through a narrow corridor, where the stench from outside mingled with the delicious aromas of cooking, and out to the back of the house. There we met an extraordinary sight: a yard filled with scores of people, all Africans, around an enormous fire. The core of the fire was hidden from view by the crowd, but the sparks it gave forth flew up into the black sky, and its glow illuminated the surroundings. The yard was bounded on the three sides other than the house from which we had emerged, by derelict buildings. Only the one directly opposite us retained a roof; through the flames that leapt up above the heads of the crowd I could see some people standing on it.

There were already a couple of musicians playing; I recognised them from the group that had been at the Clef Club on the first night that we played there. One played a horn rather like Tommy's, the other a guitar. Some of the people near them were dancing.

'Mister Jake Little, good to see you at last. Hello, boys.' The speaker was a light brown woman, who had come up behind us from the house. She wore a long purple dress decorated with tassels. 'I'm Lucille, your hostess. You set up over there where those two are playing, would you? And if there's anything you need, don't you hesitate to come ask me. There's some booze in the apartment there if you get thirsty.'

The two men who had been playing stopped when they saw us and talked to Jake while the rest of us set up the instruments. The crowd around the fire did not appear to notice this break in the entertainments, nor did they pay any attention to our preparations. But when we began to play they were electrified. Everybody was dancing. The tight groups dissolved into individual figures, moving silhouettes against the flames. The fire, I could now see, was built from huge timbers. They formed a great glowing mass at its centre. As I watched, while Tommy took a long solo, I saw some men drag another rafter from one of the derelict buildings and add it to the flaming heap. Remembering all the ruinous streets I had seen, I could envisage the whole city dragged piece by piece into the conflagration.

The people on the roof beyond the fire, their outlines inflected this way and that by the hot haze above the flames, danced as well. A woman down on the ground moved close to the flames, her hands hanging above her head. The heat seemed to draw her in. The glow of the fire on her dark brown skin was the colour of burnished brass. I was inspired by the sight, took my violin to my chin, and joined in furiously. When he heard my whirling melody behind him, Jake turned and gave me a wave of greeting.

When we had played two long, fast numbers, Tommy and I went into the house to get some drink. Behind us, Jake started a slow blues by himself.

'Quite a party, eh, John?' said Tommy as we pushed our way in the door. 'Catch those chicks doing the black bottom?' He whistled.

A man was selling bottles of spirit in one of the small rooms. We bought six, opened a couple, and took deep gulps.

'Yeah, that hits the spot,' said Tommy. 'Let's get some food before we go back.'

The small rooms and corridors were crowded with people, but

eventually we found the kitchen, where steaming plates of food were being dished out.

'What you got on the menu tonight?' asked Tommy when it came to our turn.

'We got fried fish and we got some chitterling, and blackeyed peas.'

'Gimme some of the fish, with peas on the side. My friend here'll have some too.'

The food was delicious. It fired our thirst, and we quickly finished the two bottles we had opened before going outside again. The fresh air magnified our intoxication; we stood for a while taking in the scene. Jake had moved into a faster number while we were gone, and the drummer was in the midst of a frenzied solo. The low bass drums pounded out a relentless beat, to which the cymbals held a quicksilver counterpoint. The fire raged at the heart of the dancers.

We rejoined the band, and while the battery continued we all drank from the bottles Tommy and I had brought. Jake gave us instructions, and at the end of the drummer's solo we went straight into another tune. Roars of approval went up from the crowd like the sparks from the fire that seemed to float up for miles before being quenched by the night air.

The alcohol moved within me, warmed me, then flooded up to fill my brain. My fingers continued to move over the fingerboard, my bowing arm flowed back and forth, but my mind was removed. It rolled over and over in its own orbit, it touched nothing. From this distant planet everything had a new clarity. I could trace exactly the rugged outlines of the buildings against the violent radiations of the fire. Someone was calling me. It was Jake; he was putting his trumpet in its case, and as he leant over he turned his face sideways and up at me.

'Say John, what you say we break for a while? Check out the action round here.'

'Certainly.'

Tommy was there too, laughing at something the guitarist had just said. He was at my side, clapping me on the back. And there was someone else there, a man talking to Jake and gesturing to him as he talked. There was a different hand on my back. It was

Jake's, and he was saying something to us, quickly, quietly.

'Yeah, on the house. That's what the man said. Up in the top apartment. You coming? Sure.'

The walls of the house were flaming red. They passed over us, and the world folded over into darkness and the pressing of bodies against one another. I was surrounded by words and smells. I followed Tommy's shoulder as it retreated from me. Sometimes his head turned and his face said things to me, but then the head turned back again and there was only the shoulder moving backwards through all the other shoulders. We climbed a narrow staircase. It was like the staircase I would climb as a boy to reach my room in Clerkenwell – dark and winding back and forth up the house. There were so many stairs that I imagined we were climbing right up through the night to a place beyond the stars where there would be light and clarity. But at the top there was a bare room lit by two candles placed on the floor in the centre. People were crouched around the walls.

I was sitting between Jake and Tommy with my back against the wall. The wooden boards between my legs were coarse with dirt. A low murmuring rose in the room, then died away again. There was a crack, a flame flared near me, and a tendril of sweet smoke reached my nostrils. Jake was leaning towards me, his head almost on my shoulder. His voice was low and constrained.

'Wanna hit?'

The white stick he handed me trailed smoke behind it. I put it between my lips and pulled on it. My lungs filled, and as I swallowed and blew the smoke out from my nose an involuntary shiver ran through me. I took another draught. Every muscle within me tightened and tightened, then gradually the tension was gone – not released, but dissolved, fallen apart, in the flood of a strange sensation. My body went limp. As my fingers relaxed, someone took the stick from between them.

When I opened my eyes, everything was very clear. I had been here a long time. I had always been here. The candle in front of me was the same candle that had cast a circle of light around Sergei and me on my last night aboard the ship. And at exactly that same moment as now, it guttered in the currents of air. Where was Sergei? I must leave. I tried, but my legs were heavy on the wooden planks of the deck. I would leave the ship.

Again the smoking white stick came round. I took the smoke, and felt myself move further away. Now I could see the bodies collapsed around the walls. They were moving back into the shadows, tinier and tinier until they were in focus, becoming the shadows. Now everything was clear. There were the flames and the shadows. The shadows moved on the walls, and then the flames were moving, slowly circling me, as my legs dragged beneath me. There was a hand on my arm, leading me, and a face beside me that I knew. We were going out on deck.

Only we were going down, and everything was as it had been. The fire was bigger. There was music, but we were not playing it. Tommy and I were climbing. But this was not like the stairs; we were climbing with our hands and feet. The bricks and mortar crumbled beneath us. When a chunk came off in our hands we shouted and hurled it down into the fire. We would tear the walls down as we surmounted them. Once on the roof, we looked down on the fire, the dancers, the musicians. And beyond them there was the city, with its unfolding layers of crumbling buildings and rows of orange lights.

I don't know how long Tommy and I stood on the roof. I began to think I was regaining control of my perceptions, but as soon as we moved I lost them again. We were lowering ourselves down from the roof by our hands. Everything around me was brick and pieces of metal jutting out from the wall. We let our hands go and sailed down onto the rubble beneath. I felt some metal rip through my shirt and into my chest. Lying back among the dust and bricks, we rested. Suddenly, I recalled what Mr S—— had called me: off the wall. Perhaps this was what he had meant. 'Tommy,' I cried out, 'do you think we are off the wall?' We laughed in the darkness. The music was very far away now.

When we emerged from the place in which we had landed, it was light. Dawn had come. The light was grey, and the objects in the yard appeared flat. The revellers moved around in dazed circles. The day had taken them by surprise. But it could not force them to shake off their absorption; instead, it gave the scene a dreadful clarity, like suddenly filling a claustrophobic room with light.

Jake and the others had disappeared. The music had finished, and the fire was almost dead. Tommy and I picked up our instruments and set off for home. The effects of the drug were now almost gone, and I breathed deeply the cold early-morning air. We trudged along in melancholic silence, thinking only of sleep and warmth. The streets appeared drab and familiar. The walk passed quickly and soon we found the rest and cessation that was all we wanted.

Yes, I remember how you used to look in the early morning. Rude with pink good health, you would bustle about giving your instructions to family and servants. This was your best time of the day, the time when everything lay before you. As you gave your final orders, with sparkling *bonhomie*, your horse would be saddled and waiting at the door. And then you sallied forth down Castle Hill towards the spires of the university. Every morning you took the same route: over Magdalene Bridge, down Trinity Street and across the Market Square to the Corn Exchange. There you spent your day among your ledgers and mounds of corn, wheedling and cajoling your dour, mistrustful farmers, until it was time to return again. When you got back you were tired, and seemed vaguely disillusioned, as though the day had not fulfilled everything it had promised. You retired early to bed. But the morning was the best time for you, and with the first rays of the sun you would cast off the previous night's dissatisfaction and start afresh.

I think I inherited from you that desire to go out into the world, to experience, to engage with people. You are no thinker, but I believe Mother may have been. Her wisdom was distilled in the early mornings – she would wake even earlier than you. When the rest of the house was still, she would write long letters to her closest friends. I don't think you ever knew that, for you always slept so soundly. I remember waking one October morning at dawn and coming downstairs. The mist was revealing itself thick on the grass, hiding the houses across the lane. It was cold, and Mother was sitting at the table in only her nightgown, writing a letter. She did not see me. I stood there for some time, watching

her, then crept upstairs again and sat at the window to look out
at the mist. Once or twice she read to me from the letters she
had written. The compassionate attention she lavished on each
problem of friend or family, each tangle of affairs in which you
had implicated yourself, was something I should have liked to
have inherited. Perhaps it may prove to be the case. But in
the days following my adventure at the rent party, when the
antagonism between Tommy and his siblings dragged on like a
painful ache, I found myself drawn most of all to those memories
of your eager flight into the bright morning outside.

I would think about them while looking at the sunshine outside
Tommy's window. Our all-night escapade had cast us into low
spirits. Tommy was worried that now that our engagement at the
Clef Club was over, he would not be able to find work. Eldridge's
boastfulness about his possible promotion served merely to ex-
acerbate Tommy's depression. He and I would sit for hour upon
hour in his room – he cleaning his horn and voicing his worries,
I looking out at the sunshine and occasionally taking out Mr
S——'s letter and reading it. I was beginning to feel trapped.
All my restlessness, my desire to experience, my self-disgust,
seemed to focus on this one piece of paper as a means of escape.
It struck me too that while here I was in a strange and foreign
land, I had made no attempt to discover and know my surroundings. Events had taken their course, but I had not willed them.
As a boy I had read the tales of the great discoverers, and in
those the protagonist had plunged *in media res*, had directed his
steps purposefully to the great seats of power in the land, where
he had made himself known. In my case, a chance encounter had
led me into a world where, while I had felt moments of happiness,
there was none of the thrill we gain by contact with the elevated
and powerful. Looking at Tommy slumped on his pallet, idly
whistling a tune, I could see how far I was from that world.

Thus I came to a decision to swallow my revulsion for Mr
S—— and attend him on the appointed day. Tommy's mood was
so dull and apathetic that when I asked him how I could get to
the offices on 114 W 10th Street he did not even ask why I
intended to go there. He advised me to go through the subway,
but when I told him that I would rather walk, no matter what the

distance, he drew me a map. He warned me that it would take a good two hours to get there.

On the afternoon of the day before my appointment I took an opportunity of speaking to Eldridge. He, too, was to be interviewed the following day, and the coincidence bothered me.

I left Tommy in his room, and went down to the kitchen, where Eldridge was having something to eat prior to going out on the night-shift. He was sitting at the table in his blue leggings, gobbling some bread and meat.

'Hi,' he said through a mouthful. 'Haven't seen you around for some time. You doing all right?'

'Yes, fine. I wanted to wish you luck for your interview tomorrow.'

'Thanks.' He swallowed, then went on, 'Mind you, it's nothing to do with luck. Each man on his merits.' He wiped his mouth and leant back in the chair. There was a pause.

'Have they fixed the time for your appointment?' I asked.

'Yep.' He took a swig from a bottle of beer.

'When is it?'

'Eleven o'clock, head office. I'll be there. Go there straight from work.' There was another silence.

'Actually,' I began, 'I've got an interview myself tomorrow morning.'

'For a job?'

'Perhaps.'

'Hey, that's great. Good to see you're making something of yourself. You give them all you've got.' He finished off the bottle. 'Listen, I gotta go now. We'll touch base tomorrow night, okay? It's my night off.' He picked up a small bag from beneath the table.

'Yes,' I said, 'And I hope it goes well tomorrow.'

'Thanks. 'Bye.'

I went to bed early that night in order to be up in time in the morning. But I had difficulty sleeping. Tommy had gone out somewhere, and for hours I gazed across the empty, orange-lit room. The lamp outside, on its long pole, burnt all night. With the window open one could hear the low humming it gave off. I closed my eyes, and in the darkness I could see you trotting off down Castle Hill on your horse to the Corn Exchange. At some point much later Tommy came in and collapsed on his pallet. I waited until I thought he must be asleep, then opened my eyes and looked at him. He was lying on his side with his arms splayed out. His eyes were shut, and his face was washed to a yellowish brown by the light from the window.

I must have dozed, because when I next looked out of the window the sky had lightened a bit. The lamp still burnt. I got up and crept down to the kitchen. Sitting at the table, I listened to the stillness of the house, perhaps just as Mother would sit and listen to the stillness of the early morning. Except that within me there churned an excitement, and a kind of fear. I had not got up at dawn like this since being on the ship. I looked up at the tiny window, and watched the darkness drain from the sky. Quite some time must have past while I was lost in this confused anticipation. It was time that I should be going. I checked that I had Tommy's map in my pocket, and left the house.

I walked down hundred and thirtieth to Lennox, and then along Lennox towards downtown. It was still very early, but there were many people about. The wide street was full of noise and hectic motion. I kept close to the buildings at the side of the street and walked quickly. I soon passed the barber-shop and the bar where Peewee hung out, then carried on down the straight road. For miles the landscape was the same one of crumbling buildings and casements boarded up. Then it began to change: the smaller buildings became better tended, and in among them the great towers shot straight up into the sky. The towers had no roofs, as though the builders had been unable to accept that they were finished, leaving them like that in the hope that they might one day add to them. I crossed a large park and continued down another broad street. Everything here was clean and swept. The people looked European. The buildings watched each other with a thousand eyes.

After another hour I came to W 10th Street. In amongst all the others, I found a tower with the number '114' above its entrance. Through the glass doors I could see a man in uniform looking out at me. I entered.

'Can I help you, sir?' he asked as soon as I was through the doors. The air was startlingly cool after the warmth on the street outside.

'Yes, I've come to see Mr S——.' I held out the letter for him to read. He kept his eyes fixed on the door behind me.

'Check in at the reception desk to your left, please,' he said. I walked across a vast shiny floor. In the distance there was a woman behind a low desk. The floor looked like ice. Pools of sunlight slid over it.

'Can I help you, sir?' The woman was like a painted vase.

'Yes, actually I've come to see Mr S——.' I held out the letter, but she ignored it.

'Please take a seat.' She held out one drooping hand by way of indicating a sofa behind me. I retreated to this and sat down. The woman picked something up and spoke into it, then said to me, 'Are you Mister Field?'

'Yes.' I tried to lean forward in the low, heavily padded seat.

'I'm afraid you're early. Mr S—— is busy. Would you care to wait?'

'That would be fine.'

'Thank you.' She spoke again into the thing in her hand, then put it down on the desk. She sat stock still in her seat and stared straight ahead. And since I was in front of her, she stared at me. I smiled vaguely, but she made no response. I shifted uncomfortably in my seat and she glanced away.

The great hall was as still and cold as a tomb. The sunshine flooded in through the high glass walls, but without warmth. The noise of the people on the street could not be heard. Every now and then the sound of footsteps on the hard floor echoed through the hall, as men criss-crossed it from the entrance to some metal doors at the back.

'Mister Field?' I looked back at the woman behind the table. 'Mr S—— will see you now. Twentieth floor.'

I heaved myself out of the sofa and stood for a moment, uncertainly.

'If you'd care to take the elevator.' She brought out the other hand from beneath the table and drooped it towards the metal doors.

On the twentieth floor there was a smaller hall, and another woman behind another low table.

'Can I help you, sir?'

'I've come to see Mr S——.'

'If you'd care to wait.'

The low squashy seat seemed to suck me down. I waited a few minutes, then Mr S—— appeared from around a corner.

'Good to see you, John. Really sorry to keep you waiting.'

He shook my hand strongly, pulling me up out of the seat. Then with a single smooth movement he disengaged his hand and placed it on my back in order to steer me down the corridor.

'Really glad you got my note,' he was saying, 'and decided you could make it. Knew I could count on you.' He smiled. 'And how's May? She doing all right? Marvellous. That's it, right in here.'

He propelled me through a door and closed it behind him. Talking all the while, he moved around the room so that a large desk was between us.

'Now if you'd care to sit down there, we can get down to business.'

On my side of the desk was the lowest of the seats I had yet been through. Once in it, I could barely see Mr S—— over the edge of the desk. I tried leaning forward, but the seat was designed in such a way that it tipped me back again. I gave up the struggle and sat back passively.

Mr S—— looked down at me with satisfaction.

'Okay,' he began, 'I'll give it to you straight, because I know you're a man who likes plain talking, John. I'd like to offer you a job.' He held up his hands defensively. 'Now I know you're gonna have a thousand questions to ask me before you consider an offer like that, and I'm here to answer them. But first, do you know the nature of our operation here?'

'No.'

'Information,' he replied. 'We're in the information business.' He suddenly leapt up from his seat. 'Come over here a moment, John.'

I followed him to the enormous window that made up one whole side of the room. We were high above the city. In the foreground, the glass towers rose out of the hazy heat, while beyond them an amorphous jumble of buildings spread out for as far as the eye could see. Everything looked very still at this distance. It was hard to imagine that there were people moving down there.

'Do you know what holds this city together, John?' Mr S— continued when we had stood contemplating the view for a few moments.

'Government?' I hazarded.

'Information,' he replied. 'Information's what holds this city together.'

He returned to his seat, and guided me back to mine with his hand.

'How can I put it?' he continued, with a well-rehearsed searching of the ceiling. 'You've got to imagine a great network of wires. All the information is pumping through those wires, and all those people down there, all those isolated individuals, they're all plugged individually into the system, at the end of the wires. "But where do we fit into this?" you're asking yourself. Well, we're at the heart of it. We're pumping the information down those wires.'

'But where does the information come from?' I put in.

'From our clients. That could be anyone. Hell, John, *you* could have some information fed through the system – provided you had the money, of course. Our clients are anyone who can afford to pay. That's democracy. That's freedom. We just put those transmission slots on the market and they go crazy to get them. It's a seller's market, cause what we're selling is a very valuable commodity. What we're selling is *access into people's heads.*'

'But where do the clients get it from?'

'The money?'

'The information.'

'We can't worry about that, John,' he said firmly. 'We're just in the transmission business. Our job is to make sure that all those people down there,' he waved an arm at the window, 'are plugged in. It's their inalienable right. I'll tell you, John: it makes me mad when I see groups left out of the information community. That's why I work closely with the CAU, trying to give them a higher profile. We have to access them into the network. Okay, call it extending the market if you like. But the point is that those minority groups musn't be left out. We've gotta embrace them. Which brings me to you.'

He leant towards me, smiling. I tried sitting up in my seat.

'You're probably asking yourself by now, "This guy, he like offers me a job right away, but what's he getting out of it, what's his angle?" Am I right? Well, it's the same as with the CAU. You're on the outside, and I just want to give you a helping hand to come on in here and join us. That's all. I've done the same for other immigrants. Now, you must have a lot of questions for me.'

I looked at the window, on which the sunlight spread a dazzling reflection. I had concentrated hard when Mr S—— had been speaking, but when I tried to recall his words for the purpose of making a response, it was as though they had floated out through the glass.

'Well, I have a couple of questions for you, John,' he continued. 'Are you still living up there with May's family?'

'Yes.'

He looked down at his desk, frowning. 'I've gotta say it, John, your life's been pretty screwy here, hasn't it?'

'Perhaps,' I replied lamely.

'Hanging out with those musicians,' he continued, tracing a line on a piece of paper before him with his pen. Then he looked up at me with an appealing smile. 'Look, John, you can stay at my place for a while, till you get yourself sorted out. I'm sure Jean wouldn't mind. Fact, she'd love quizzing you about old England. She adores all that stuff. You'd be quite a social asset, you know that?'

'It's very kind of you, but I'm happy with May's family.'

'Well, okay,' he said with the same defensive gesture of his hands, 'but you will let me know if you change your mind, won't you?'

'Yes.'

'Good.' He smiled and beat a celebratory tattoo with his fingers on the edge of the table. 'As far as the job goes, I'm gonna give you an assignment in Direct Access Sales. You'll be happy there, John: it's the cutting edge.'

'What will I be doing?' I asked eagerly.

'Two things. You'll operate an auction to fill the information slots, then package and transmit using your VDU. It all happens pretty fast – it has to. If you're afraid of burn-out you should tell me now, John.'

'No,' I said firmly.

He looked at me with admiration. 'Great,' he said. We smiled at each other. 'Can you start tomorrow?'

'Sure.'

He pressed something on the desk before him, and a woman came through the door. She led me down to the entrance of the building, where I stood for a few moments, blinking. The sunlight was funnelled down between the buildings and magnified by the reflecting windows; the sky seemed to be all around one. I looked along the street at the stream of passing faces and the brittle crust that clattered beneath their feet. The surfaces of things burst at me in the sharp light. It was hot.

I started walking back up the street the way I came. I walked slowly, nudged along by the crowd. I reached the park and started across it. But half way across, feeling tired and relieved to be away from the people, I lay down on the grass. The sun seemed to fill everything with a hot emptiness. I half dozed for a few minutes, feeling this hollowness grow inside me. I felt utterly disconnected from past and present. I opened my eyes and sat up. The park was very large, and the roar of noise from the streets that surrounded it was hardly audible. The tops of the tall buildings in the distance rode above the trees like ships on a green sea. I lay back again and fell asleep.

When I woke I could sense immediately that some hours had passed. The air was cooler and the light less intense. It was evening. I sat up and looked around. There were people running everywhere, they weaved between the trees and across the great expanses of mown grass. There was no panic or confusion. They were simply running around. I got up and started walking. By the time I reached Lennox and started heading along it to uptown, it was getting dark.

When I turned into hundred and twentieth I saw Eldridge coming in the other direction, from the railroad. We greeted each other and went into the house together. He was unusually quiet: 'Fine evening, ain't it?' was all he said to me. His head was bowed, so that I could not see his expression. A light was burning in the front room of the house, the room where I had first met Tommy. We entered, and stood for a moment in the dark hallway. From behind the door came the sounds of singing and laughter. Eldridge reached forward and opened it.

It was a second or two before the occupants became aware of our presence in the doorway. Jake was sitting in a chair playing a guitar; Tommy was crouched beside him waving his horn in the air; and May was behind them, with one hand on each of their shoulders. They looked up, and the singing stopped. The air was heavy with the smell of drink, and there were empty bottles on the bare wooden floor. Jake, after taking us in, looked back down at the instrument and continued playing, though in a more subdued tone. May moved around the chair and stood in front of Jake and Tommy as if protecting them. Eldridge walked past her into the room.

'Give us some of that beer, will you?' he said, as he slumped down into a chair.

'Yeah, give these guys some beer,' said May.

Tommy handed round some bottles.

We all swigged except Jake, who continued a meandering melody.

'Well?' said May, looking down at Eldridge.

'Well what?'

'What do you think?'

'Who says I can think?' He looked around him and underneath the chair on which he sat. 'I never heard anyone say I can think.'

There was a snort of laughter from Tommy.

'C'mon, Eldridge,' said May. 'Don't get wise with me. What happened? Do you think you got it?'

'What do *you* think?' he said quietly, and looked at the floor.

There was a long silence. Jake's melody had almost trailed away to nothing.

'You mean you didn't get it?'

'What do you think?' he said again, quieter.

'Who did?'

'Some honky.' There was another long pause. 'Gave that job to some fresh-faced kid with half the experience I've got. "Guess you won't be getting uppity again for a while." That's what Joe says.'

As he was talking, a low murmur started up from Tommy. It was a song, a repeated refrain, that Jake accompanied on the guitar:

> *Oh, they picked poor robin clean.*
> *Oh, they picked poor robin clean*
> *They tied poor robin to a stump*
> *Lord, they picked all the feathers*
> *Round from robin's rump*
> *Oh, they picked poor robin clean.*

The song was like a dirge, but with an absurdly exaggerated comic tone. May began to smile, then looked anxiously at Eldridge. Eldridge listened for a moment, puzzled, then laughed and began to sing as well. They all joined in. But somehow I could not. I stood near the door, drinking nervously. When the song had died down, May looked over at me.

'Lost your voice, John?' she said.

I looked around for somewhere to sit down, but all the seats were taken. Jake was continuing to play the tune of the song on the guitar.

'Your day go okay?' she said.

'Yes, I suppose so,' said I

'Saw Mike, did you?'

'Yes.'

'He offer you a job?'

'Yes.'

'And you took it?'

'Yes. But . . .'

'Hear that, you guys,' she said triumphantly, turning to the others. They looked at her uncertainly. 'We should be celebrating for John here, not grieving 'cause Eldridge didn't get a job he should have got.' She looked back at me. 'Now ain't that something? Eldridge sweats it out for years on the railroad and can't get promotion, and you arrive here and land yourself a nice job downtown just like that.' She snapped her fingers.

'Ah, leave it, May,' said Tommy.

'Now I wonder how that can be?' she persisted.

'C'mon, May, give the guy a break,' said Eldridge. 'What he do wrong? He got himself a job. Can't see the harm in that.'

'Yeah, he fixed himself up all right,' she said.

'But I didn't seek the job,' I put in. 'Mr S—— was insistent, and it . . .'

'You poor son of a bitch,' cried May. 'We really sympathise, don't we, guys?' She turned to the others.

'Shit, let's go out and get a drink,' said Tommy. 'It's getting too heavy in here.' Jake, Tommy and Eldridge got up and made for the door. May and I stayed facing each other in the centre of the room.

'We'll be out in the street if you two're coming,' said Tommy as they were leaving.

The door slammed, and May and I were left alone. She looked me steadily in the eye.

'You doing all right now, aren't you? Strikes me you don't need us any more. Landed right on your feet, hit the ground running, you have.'

'But I didn't plan any of this, I assure you.'

'No, you're a real innocent, aren't you? Just landed in your lap like a juicy fruit falling straight out of the sky. You know I could see this coming a long way off, at the CAU meeting. You and Mike huddled up together in the corner there, sticking together like a couple of leeches. Couple of white bloodsuckers.'

'But I thought Mr S—— was your friend, your colleague in the CAU?'

'Yeah, he's with the CAU. But that doesn't mean I'm blind or stupid, does it?'

'Then I may as well tell you,' I said, 'that my motive in approaching Mr S—— was entirely different to what you imagine. Actually, I was worried about your welfare. I was worried that you might be putting yourself in a position of danger by your involvement in the CAU. I wanted to find out more about how things stood, and I thought the best way of doing that would be to glean it from Mr S——. My sole concern was for your welfare.'

For a few moments she just gazed at me. She was almost shaking with rage.

'What gives you the right?' she yelled. 'That's what I want to know. What makes you think you got the right to come barging in here thinking you know what's best for me. You're like all the rest. You think I'm some kind of dumb animal can't look after itself. I can't think for myself? That what you think? Eh?'

'No.'

'Well? That all you've got to say for yourself? Besides, what do you know about any of this? You must have a real big opinion of yourself.'

'It was Tommy. He asked me to do it. He was worried about you. He said I'd be able to find out what the position was.'

'If you want to drag my brother into this: well, I think he's as dumb as you. The two guys get together and decide that the little woman can't look after herself in the rough man's world. So the thing needs checking out. The both of you are such idiots, I'd laugh if I wasn't so mad. Well, let me tell you something, Mister John Field. I can do okay without your assistance. And it looks like you can do without ours. So you can sleep here tonight and then take your bags and clear off downtown in the morning where you belong. I'm sure Mike'll fix you up with your own kind.'

May's anger had infected me. With a mixture of confusion and rage, I blurted out in reply: 'Actually he did offer me somewhere to stay, and I refused and said I would prefer to stay here. But I think under the circumstances I will gladly take up his offer. Yes, gladly.'

'Well, I won't have to waste time worrying how you're getting on,' she said, walking past me to the door. 'I'll rest easy as far as you're concerned, Mister Field.'

'Furthermore,' I added, 'I think you would do well to be suspicious of Mr S—— . . .'

'Listen, Mister Field,' she interrupted me. 'Nothing you say gonna hurt me. Right?'

With that she slammed the door and marched along the corridor to the kitchen, where I could hear her banging pots around. Tears of anger and confusion and self-pity pricked my eyes. I wiped them away and went outside onto the street. The others had gone. I stood there for a long time and thought about looking for them. But I know that I would never find them. The city had never seemed so dark. I stared up into a night sky that was as black as pitch. My anger was hot inside me. I stretched my mouth open, but nothing came out. An old African couple glanced warily at me as they passed.

You will understand from my account the feelings I entertained concerning this last encounter with May. I had been cowardly and dishonest in what I had told her. If I had but explained to her my true confusions – that since childhood I had looked for escape, only to find fresh entrapment – then things might have been different. But I had not had the spirit to say that. I was filled with the worst self-loathing, the kind one spits out again as venom, as hatred for all and everything. I stood in the street. It had been many hours since I had risen; fatigue was weakening me to dark emotions. I went back into the house and up to Tommy's room, where I lay down on my pallet and closed my eyes. The darkness was a relief; it had depth. I crawled into it.

Through the darkness there moved like a snake through a deep pool a new and sudden hatred. I hated May, Tommy, Eldridge and their mother for being unimportant. I loathed them for their inconsequentiality. I was a traveller from a place of which they knew nothing. They were blind. They were stupid enough to misunderstand me even when I was among them, to misinterpret somehow my honest actions. Their lives would stagnate in this run-down house and be swept over by the great tide of history. Mine would extend itself in all directions from Mr S——'s glass tower in the sky, and encompass the whole city. I hated them as a group and I hated them individually – Tommy for his indolence, May for her questions, Eldridge for his failure, and their mother for having borne them.

At some point in the night I heard Tommy stumble into the room, but I kept my eyes clenched shut and followed my tortuous thoughts. I longed for the daylight. When it came, I packed my few possessions into my sack, took a last look at Tommy splayed out asleep on his pallet, and left the house.

*   *   *

During the days that followed, summer reached its boiling point. The air was damp and heavy. One hardly knew how the sun managed to blast its heat through the atmosphere. But blast it did. It was tremendously hot.

At the height of the day, W 10th Street was like a hundred rivers converging, a whirlpool of humanity. From high up in the office it was an interesting sight. Mr S—— liked to stand with me at the window and look down on it. He had a pleasant game that he would play with me. He liked to pick out an individual current of people as it formed, trace its course as it swelled, then watch it come apart as a new one materialised. This gave him endless delight. The crowd was indeed an ever-changing entity. But down on the street there was precious little room at all for thought. Many of the people had stripped till they were almost naked, and as one was jostled through the crowd one could feel a cold and clammy arm pressed against one's side, or find oneself pushed up against a sweaty back. As one struggled to make a passage, the chest would begin to heave and the heart to pound. Gasping for breath, the lungs were clogged with heat and bad-tasting white smoke. The street was like a dry river-bed, a crevice through which there moved thousands of stamping, choking animals.

Up in the office it was clean and cool. On my first morning a woman explained to me how I was to do my job. She was bored. As she talked, her gaze flitted about her and out of the window to the city below. When she addressed me, she looked past me and spoke loudly, as though she were addressing someone at the other end of the room.

'You doing anything for lunch, John?' she said when we had finished.

'No.'

'I'll show you this place a couple of blocks away if you like.'

'Thank you very much.'

'That's all right.'

We went downstairs. When I opened the door onto the street, the noise of machines rang my skull like a bell. She took me to a small coffee-house, where we perched on high stools in a long line of customers. She talked about other places where she had eaten.

'You been to that Italian place round the corner, John?'

'No.'

'God, you should *go* there. It's really . . . *you know.*'

She talked about the clothes she wore, the plays she'd seen, the men she knew. When we had eaten, and were getting up to leave, she said, 'We should do a lunch again soon. What do you say?'

She was not in my office the next day. She had moved to another department, and thereafter I only saw her in the distance across the polished floor of the entrance hall – except once, when she appeared alongside me as I was waiting for the sliding metal doors to open. We entered the room together. This was the room that took me to my office; it sang to me and made me sick. As we stood opposite each other inside it, the mirrors reflecting us a hundred-fold, she chewed like the woman in the bank. When the room stopped and the doors opened, she smiled again and walked off in the other direction. That was the last I saw of her.

I found it hard to establish contact with anyone at work. My presence was absorbed without a ripple on the surface of the office's orderly routine. They knew my name, and when they passed me in the corridor they nodded and said, 'Hi, John.' And they held their heads high, like courtiers. Once or twice, I attempted to detain someone and engage them in conversation. They heard me out politely, then glanced at the watch they all wore strapped around their wrists, and said, 'Well, John, Time is Money,' or some such. Mr S—— liked to say that too. As well as the watches, there were clocks on all the walls. They didn't tick like yours used to, but the machines in my office clicked and hummed constantly. I listened to them, but I couldn't tell what they were saying. I stared at their hard, shiny surfaces and thought about the immobilised faces of those I met in the corridors.

The hours passed slowly, filling the days with their hot vacuity. I talked into a machine, and the machine talked back in different voices. They were always the same voices, but I never learnt their names. They were only media for the money they could offer. When Mr S—— had said that I would be conducting auctions, I had pictured in my mind a sea of faces shouting and gesticulating at me. Instead, there were six voices. They whispered in my ear like lovers. I felt flattered and seduced. But then, as Mr S—— had said, I had something valuable to offer them: access into people's heads. I began to encourage them, to urge them to higher bids that my vanity might be stroked some more. And, as I pressed my ear to the machine to catch their breathy voices, they responded. They were all men. Unable to hear each other, they spoke to me in low, private voices. One by one, as the price of the communication slot rose, they dropped out of the auction, until there would be just two of them talking numbers to me.

The achievement of the highest price, the end of the auction, was almost an anti-climax. The voices fell silent, the lines were closed, and it only remained for me to transmit the information. The slot was filled. For a few moments, the numbers and facts appeared before me at the centre of the network. Then I sent them on their way. They were dispersed. Sometimes I would sit back and try to imagine the stories behind the information, but I couldn't. They had been skimmed off the surface of life. Who knows if they were true? They seemed weightless. So I would get back to work, fiddle with the buttons, and squint furiously at the green words and figures on the screen. It gave me a headache. It reminded me of you, bent at your desk in the counting-house, while Mother and I breathed the summer air at Dunwich beach.

Mr S—— was quite amenable to my staying with him. He expressed no surprise that I should have changed my mind on the matter; it seemed to be what he had been expecting. His attitude towards me was almost paternal – which I was glad of, for I had hopes of advancement through his offices. In those first days in the glass tower I was full of ambition. If I could but gain greater responsibility in Mr S——'s organisation, I thought – which, as he himself said, was more important to the city than government – then who knows where my advancement might end? As I looked across the sparkling array of downtown buildings, I was lifted to dreams of power. From high up in the office it seemed to be within my grasp. But power is a cloudy thing. The

enjoyment of it can evaporate in a moment, the desire for it no
more substantial than an itch on the brain.

But an itch, though insubstantial, does absorb the mind. I was
most attentive to Mr S——, and spent much time with him that
I might learn from him. Wherein lay his power? That was the
question I asked myself ceaselessly. I studied him from every
angle, but I could see nothing. He had assurance – but was that
a symptom or a cause? Everything about him attested to his
power, and others bore witness to it. Yet these things were like
properties hung on an empty staging, for the power itself was
nowhere. I wonder if I didn't look at you in that way sometimes,
Father.

My every evening with Mr S—— was the same. At the
appointed time, I got into the singing room and was moved to his
office. There I waited in the squashy seat before the painted lady
while Mr S—— finished his business. When he was done, he
came out and drove me home. The uptown streets that had
become familiar to me sped noiselessly by beyond the windows.
Mr S—— tapped his fingers impatiently.

There is no end or boundary to the city. It merely thins out,
becomes more expansive and confident, until the large houses
are spreading themselves most lavishly across the low hills. This
is the suburbs.

'Boy, it's good to get home,' Mr S—— would say as we pulled
up the drive and stopped. Mrs S—— would be coming out of the
house to greet us, her arms and neck hung with precious stones
and metal. She rattled as she moved. Her skin was leathery
brown from exposure to the sun, and her cheeks were as tight
as a drum. Once we had been ushered into the cool of the house,
Mr S—— would slump in a chair and pass a shaking hand across
his brow, as though he had narrowly escaped an accident. 'Good
to get home,' he would say, again.

His wife would pour us drinks. Clear liquid in a clear glass. It
was so cold that it stung the teeth.

In the evenings, Mr and Mrs S—— and myself sat around the
table and ate dinner. While Mr S—— concentrated on his food,
his wife asked me about life in England. She seemed fascinated,
for she had an inexhaustible supply of questions. But as time

went on I had a strange feeling that she was not taking in what I said, or even thought I was mad. Mr S—— would not speak until he had filled his stomach, but then he would hold the stage. As the insects whirred in the hot night outside, and the lights above us hummed and buzzed, Mr S—— would discourse at length on his network and the philosophy thereof.

'We're moving apart,' he would say, 'as we realise our individuality and liberate ourselves. Maximising individual freedom, you see, means a world of increased disorganisation. And where there's autonomous initiative, you need to maximise the information flow. That's where we come in. We used to be taught that the efficiency of a system is measured by the amount of productive work it does, right? Well, forget that. That's obsolete. What you've gotta look at now is the amount of internal motion in the system. That's your information flow, which is the only thing that's gonna keep the whole caboodle together.'

When Mr S—— flagged, his wife would interject with heart-felt questions about my state of mind like, 'You must be *very* excited about working in the organisation?' or 'What, for you, is the single most exciting aspect of working with data?' I was driven half out of my wits with boredom and incomprehension.

Mr S——, perhaps gauging my mood, would exhort me, 'Yeah, you've come into the business at just the right time. This is quite a moment in our development, and we're all proud to be a part of it.' He smiled shyly. 'I probably shouldn't be telling you this, John, but we're moving into space. That's the next step. We've got ourselves an empire to build, and by God we're gonna do it.' His head shook with resolution.

I developed a strange habit when Mr S—— was talking to me of pressing my hand onto the shiny surface of the table that separated us. Once I had pressed it in, I would lift my hand slowly to admire the sweaty impression my palm had made. I don't know why I did this, but it seemed to give me some satisfaction.

Perhaps it was a covert rebellion against Mr S——. I certainly never disagreed with him openly, for the good reason that I could make neither head nor tail or what he said. Once, however, I did venture to question him. He had been talking, as he liked to do, about images and profiles.

'The projection of image,' he said, 'is vital to the communication across difference. That's where we come in, John, 'cause it takes professionals like us to form and project those images. Pretty soon the day will come when direct speech will be a thing of the past.'

'Would that not be a shame?' I said.

He smiled condescendingly. 'Well, maybe, John. But you know you've got to start dealing with the world as it is, not how you'd like it to be. That's the necessity of things.'

His last phrase had a curious effect on me. I began thinking about you, for I had once heard you use those very same words. I was seventeen at the time, and had come back from London to Cambridge on hearing from you that your friend Mr Harnham might have a position for me as surgeon aboard one of his ships out of Bristol. I knew nothing of the slave trade, and it seemed to me inconceivable that one as young and inexperienced as I should act as physician aboard a ship. When I voiced my doubts you laughed.

'Nonsense, my boy,' you said. 'The thing you must understand about a slaver is that standards are, shall we say, a little less stringent. No, if you wish to enter into a career as a physician, I would say that this would provide an invaluable opportunity to gain experience and experiment. Believe me, when you see the condition of those poor wretches you'll realise that nothing you might inadvertently do could make their sufferings any worse.'

'But is it not wrong to treat them so?' I asked.

You laughed. 'Now you're touching upon general considerations,' you said, 'which I always think are best left to philosophers and such. We're men for the practicalities. To be sure, they should be treated as well as possible, but the slave trade is a hard business, and unquestioning discipline requires hard measures. As for whether the trade itself is justified – why, it's hardly a question. Slavery is commerce, the most important commerce. And not an argument in the world will broach the supremacy of commerce. It's the necessity of things.'

If this reminiscence was odd, then what happened next was yet stranger, and not a little unpleasant. For as Mr S——, invigorated by my lack of reply, began to expand his thesis, his

voice seemed to become your voice. I was so confused that I
could no longer be sure whether it was still Mr S—— I was
hearing, or your voice talking in my head. Indeed, the two became
one. I tried to speak. But this voice, resounding across my past
and present, throttled and silenced me. Perhaps Mrs S—— was
right, and I was going mad.

But please, Father, do not conclude that I think you resembled
him. We each of us collect the things against which we rebel
under one head, and associate them the one with the other. I
rebelled against you, and fled from home at the tender age of
thirteen, to escape the tick of the clock on the counting-house
wall. It cost me dearly to return to seek your help at seventeen.
I had rebelled also because you were, quite simply, my father.
You had given me everything, and none of it had I asked for.

As the days passed, blurring together, the ambitions which had
drawn me to Mr S—— faded. And in truth, there was no other
reason for my association with him and his wife. So all that was
left was the routine of drifting backwards and forwards between
downtown and the suburbs, like a leaf that swings to and fro on
the air as it falls. This feeling of rootlessness sapped my spirits.
For in one important respect I take after Mother: I only feel
happy in the company of those I know and trust. Even as a child,
I noticed how the circle of Mother's acquaintances contracted,
until there was just family and her three oldest friends. I believe
these were the only people she met in the years before she died.
In those days with Mr S——, I thought of Mother much, and
pondered on the similarities between us. I came to realise that I
had always kept a respectful distance between myself and those
I came across casually. I had never previously noticed this characteristic in myself, because my attention was always on an intimate
friendship, such as Sergei's. But now, without this acceptance,
the distance I kept from others took on a life of its own. As I
went to and from the office with Mr S——, I began to watch and
criticise people's reaction to me. It struck me that they were not
seeing me, that they were simply trusting to my good character
and passing on. By taking so much for granted, by desiring above
all that those I met should think well of me, I had allowed a great
chasm to open up between myself and my surroundings. I looked

at the people, and it seemed to me that they smiled a lot. The more I scrutinised them, the more they dissolved before my eyes, leaving only a bland smile. But why, and for whom, were they smiling? I could not tell.

The room in which I worked was so clear as to seem airless. A hot mist shrouded the streets, but I was far above it. The glass walls of the building seemed to let the whole world in in a flood of light. Often I would be overcome by giddiness, and pace about my crystal cage. I had become obsessed with this thought of the distance between myself and my surroundings. I developed the absurd suspicion that through my transparent confines I was being watched by the whole city. As the light and the world flooded into the room, I retreated to ever darker and more obscure corners of my soul, until all contact seemed to have been lost between the stiff, actorish body that moved around, and the small, desperate voice within.

Off to one side of the building in which I was housed was an even higher glass tower. Looking up at the top of this structure, and then down again at the ground far below, I was invaded by a hollow sense of limitless space, and reminded invidiously of Mr S——'s abstract ambitions. Looking down, I could see workers scurry like ants over a network of girders and ladders, building yet another tower. Monsieur Yepanchin once described to me the construction of St Petersburg. As he told me that terrible story – of how thousands had perished, hacking through the ice and carrying stone across the frozen marshes – my gentle teacher wept at the thought of so many lives being sacrificed to the vanity and ambition of the Czar. Now I wondered who had ordered the building of these glass palaces? To whose glory were they? My mind skated and slid. I could gain no grip.

I focused on one worker in particular. He was climbing down a ladder, checking his footing carefully as he descended. The danger he felt was as direct and real as the sensation of the wooden rungs pressing into the soles of his feet. I sympathised with him in his uneasiness. But the ladder on which I stood was invisible. My feet found no footing, and I knew not where I might fall. Only my dizziness testified to the void beneath me.

When I left Tommy's house, I thought I was to enter into the real life of the city. But in truth I now felt more removed from it. My very sensations seemed to slide away from beneath me like an over-polished floor. I was cast adrift without moorings. My office was at the corner of the downtown tower. Only two of the walls were made of glass, but sometimes it seemed that I was entirely surrounded by the summer sky, and that I was floating helplessly out into the blue nothingness. I took to calling it the 'blue room'.

Then, gradually, a great peace stole up on me. Inside, I was as empty as the blank blueness that surrounded my office in the sky. When Mr S—— and his wife left me for a couple of days for their 'retreat' in the mountains, and I was alone in their house, a serenity descended that was so intense as to be like a constant noise. The air was so still, the silence so present, that I thought perhaps the world had come to a stop and all the people quitted it.

The suburb was always quiet. But for those couple of days it was especially so. The house was cool, so I spent much of the time indoors, trying to remember scraps of melody and wishing I had a violin with me. Occasionally I would venture outside and walk around the lawn that surrounded the house. Mr and Mrs S——'s neighbours seemed to have gone to their retreats as well. Only the dogs were left. Penned behind the high metal fences of their separate lawns, they had the place to themselves. There was one on the lawn of the house next door. I watched as it raised its head and barked. It sent its howl out through the hot air over the metal fence. In the distance, far over a leafy hill, came a reply. The afternoon was as slow as a thick liquid. I lay down on the short, hard grass, and listened to the dogs barking to each other across the empty suburb. It was a melancholy sound.

When evening came, I went back inside and prepared some food. And when I was fed, I lay down on my bed and tried to sleep. But my mind was rebelling obscurely against the quiet of place. I opened my eyes, and the soft sunset beyond the window became hard-edged and active. Something surged in my skull. I closed my eyes again.

*　　*　　*

I was like a bubble, floating about with an emptiness inside me. A few days later I burst. It all began as I was completing my fourth auction of the morning. The slot had been sold, and I had turned to the screen to process the green information. I thought all the clients had closed their lines. But then I noticed a faint crackle in the air, which indicated that a line was still open. I turned round, and as I did so, one of the voices said, 'John?'

'Hello?' I replied.

'Just a quick word,' the voice continued with quiet rapidity. 'I wouldn't normally do this. Just to say I'll be leaving at noon today. Amy and I are having a dinner party. See you then.' There was a click as the line closed.

For a few moments I sat back and gazed at the machine in amazement. It was Mr S——'s voice. But that voice, which I had only just recognised, had been taking part in all the auctions. What would Mr S—— be doing trying to buy his own communications slots? The question bothered me for the rest of the morning.

At noon I went up to Mr S——'s office. He was expecting me. As we drove across town, forcing a passage through the sweaty crowds on the streets, he told me about his success that morning in acquiring new audiences. The network was growing, and he was in excellent spirits. For a while I thought he was going to say nothing about what had happened that morning. But then he exclaimed, 'God, John, you know it feels *good*. I can't wait to tell Amy about all of this. Are we gonna have a good time tonight? I mean, are we gonna celebrate? It was against all the rules me doing that this morning. But then I made the rules, so I guess I can break them.' He laughed, and slammed his palm against the steering wheel. 'Seriously though, John, I don't know what the hell came over me, breaching security like that. A rush of blood to the head, I guess. I don't have to tell you what kind of stuff would hit the fan if it got out that . . . you know . . .' He blew through his teeth.

'Yes indeed.' I nodded and shook my head, pretending to know exactly what he was talking about. He changed the subject, and I was left none the wiser.

When we got back to the suburbs, Mr S—— rushed into the house to tell Mrs S—— the good news. She was in the kitchen, preparing for the supper party. By the time I had ambled in the door, they were clapping their hands together and jumping up and down. I walked on past them and lay down on the lawn. It was hotter than ever. I shut my eyes against the glaring sun and saw red. I felt exhausted.

Later, I was woken by the door of the house banging.

'You'll get burnt, John,' said Mrs S——, 'lying in the sun like that.'

I opened my eyes, raised my head, and watched her approach me across the lawn. She wore short trousers and a vest that hung loosely about her chest. Her hair was tied up.

'Hi,' she said when she was standing over me. 'I'm going jogging. I try and do it every day. You should come too. Do you jog? I found it's become a really important part of my life. I couldn't do without it.'

I made no reply.

'We're so lucky having the beach close by.'

I looked up. 'Are we near the sea?' I asked.

'Sure, the ocean's only about a mile away. I run along the beach there in the evenings. Sometimes in the early morning. Why don't you come and take a look?' She shifted her weight from one foot to another.

I thought for a moment. 'No thank you.'

'Okay. See you,' she said, and bounced away across the grass.

I sat up. It was cooler now. I sniffed the breeze, and imagined for a moment that it was flavoured with salt.

When Mrs S—— returned she bathed, then I helped her polish the silver in preparation for the evening's festivities. Mr S—— was at work in his study. As the cutlery twinkled in the last rays of daylight, Mrs S—— gave me information about the guests who would be coming. The profession of each was ranked according to three criteria: it should be profitable, but not vulgar; interesting, but not esoteric; and socially useful, but never dangerous to the established order. More importantly, however, her friends had to be successful in whatever they did. Otherwise they would not be topics of conversation. Listening to her, I was overcome by a numbing depression of the spirits, a sense that the whole of life is a meaningless waste.

But I should not speak badly of Mrs S——, for she was most kind to me. She had laundered my waistcoat and breeches so well that all the sea salt and city dirt had been washed out of them, and their original colours were restored. She had polished the buttons of them till they shone like the knives and forks. I stood before her, and she asked me nicely if I wouldn't assist her later by handing round the wine for her guests. I was to be a butler.

In the evening, when the guests arrived, I took their coats and led them through to the dining-room, where Mr and Mrs S—— received them. I felt invisible. When I moved between them dispensing wine, they hardly shifted to let me pass. When they were seated at table, I continued to flit from glass to glass like a bee visiting flowers. In the kitchen, when I left them to fetch fresh bottles, I swigged on the wine to make myself drunk.

It was on my return from one of these excursions that I was first noticed by the company.

'Like John here,' exclaimed Mr S——, casting his arm in my direction as I approached the table. I stopped. He was in the midst of an oration on the subject of the network. 'John here is one of the strongest forces in our sales team.' The company turned and looked at me with interest. 'Isn't that right, John?'

In reply I bowed, staggering slightly to one side as I did so like an actor staying in character at the curtain call. The company at table laughed good-naturedly, and I hurried forward to replenish their glasses.

All their conversation concerned their professional success. Mr S——'s peroration was on the subject of his network's absorption of the CAU. This theme was taken up by a large gentleman at the other end of the table.

'I think it's real important to patronise minorities,' he said, wiping his mouth with a cloth. 'Take my company, we've just contracted a bunch of black musicians. Very good they are too, I'm informed by my experts. And I'll tell you, I was real happy to take them on. A deal like that is progressive and profitable.' At the word 'progressive' he held out one hand, and at 'profitable' the other. Now he brought the two hands together and, grinning round at the others, interlocked his fingers.

I meanwhile, fatigued by drink, had slumped in a chair at the side of the room. Nobody seemed to notice my absence from table. I had a bottle in my hand, and swigged mindlessly on it now and again. I felt as though I were in the singing room going up to my office. All it needed was some singing. So I began to sing, then I laughed because it was ridiculous that Mr and Mrs S—— and all their guests should be squashed into the singing room. Two of the guests heard me laugh, and turned round to join in. They thought I was laughing at something they had said. It was only then I realised that everybody else was as drunk as I.

I continued to drink. Later, when all the guests had gone and Mrs S—— had retired to bed, I cleared the dirty plates and cutlery into the kitchen. Mr S—— stood to one side and supervised me. I staggered to and fro beneath the bright, buzzing lights in a fog of inebriation. My eyes, glazed by the brightness, were like the hard, reflecting surfaces of the machines in the kitchen. Mr S—— switched the machines on, and they roared with pain. I fell to my knees, the dishes crashing around me. I wanted to claw open those brittle shells and release whatever was inside. My arms swam through the unforgiving white light. As I slumped to the floor, I began thinking for some reason of London, and remembered the narrow brick streets receding through the silent darkness.

Mr S——'s hand was on my shoulder.

'Why don't you get to bed, John?' he was saying. 'I'll finish up in here.'

I looked round. He was stooping over me, smiling at me. It was as though nothing had happened. The machines still roared, the lights still shone. He put a hand beneath my arm, and half-pushed, half-dragged me towards the door.

'You look bushed, John,' he said. 'Pace too tough?' He laughed.

I stood up and detached myself from him.

'Another thing,' he said, already turning away from me. 'Amy'll give you a ride down to the station tomorrow. You can get the train to work. I've got to go out of town for the day.'

*   *   *

I had never been on the train before, but the thought did not excite me. Even next morning, when I was in it, it didn't interest me. My head was still heavy with drink, and the windows were so dirty that I could see practically nothing through them. I slumped deep in the cushioned seat and stared at my boots. The train entered a tunnel. I looked through the grime at the thundering blackness. It went on and on, pitching and rumbling forward. I could no longer tell if we were moving. Perhaps the carriage was standing in the darkness and simply vibrating? Then it shot out of the other end. I leapt up, realising suddenly how fast I was moving. The window, I noticed, was a sash. I grabbed the handle and slid it down. A breeze brushed my face and blew down through the empty carriage. The train was speeding down an avenue of trees. As it disturbed the air, the leaves danced in the sunlight. Remembering what Mrs S—— had said, I strained to see the ocean. Once, when there was a gap in the trees, I thought I saw the glitter of light on water. The smell of seaweed touched my nostrils. I was filled by an unaccountable excitement. The wheels, as they rounded a bend, seemed to pluck laughter from the tracks as though they were the strings of a violin.

Soon afterwards we stopped. Hot air hissed from beneath the carriage. I watched a single leaf shimmer in the wind then slowly come to rest. Everything was silent and still. The warm air from outside flooded in through the open window. I listened to the carriage tick and wheeze as it wound down. Eventually it fell into a deep and inert silence. I listened. There was nothing but an ill-defined sound of human activity further down the train.

We had stopped a little way outside the city. I leaned out of the window to have a look. Up ahead, the track disappeared in a straight line towards downtown, while in the other direction it curved away through the trees. The scene was so still as to become fixed, like a painting. The sunlight cast deep, cool shadows beneath the wheels. Occasionally a breeze flicked up the leaves, showing their pale underparts. The only clouds in the sky were far, far off above the horizon. Perhaps that was where the coast was. Here it was as still as a hinge that remains motionless while all about it moves.

I sat back again and listened. The noise from further along the train had been continuing all this time, perhaps even getting louder. It was the scraping and jangling of metal on stone. As it drew level with my carriage, I looked back down across the aisle, and through the dusty window I could see some black, wiry hair. The scraping stopped, and the head bobbed down for a moment. It reappeared and the scraping recommenced. I rushed across to the window, and there was Eldridge, dragging a shovel behind him. I knocked on the window. He started and looked about alertly, then saw me and pointed in recognition. He shouted to me, but I could not hear, so I dashed along to the door of the carriage.

'Eldridge, how extraordinary to meet you,' I cried.

'You appeared out of nowhere, man,' he laughed, stumbling towards me. 'I was just walking along thinking about what I might be having for dinner, and this face I know jumps up in the window of the train. Walking along thinking about nothing, and you appears out of nowhere!' He laughed again.

'How are you? How is everything?'

'Okay. Tommy gotta contract with a record company. He's gonna cut a record. Got me an interview with them too, for a job as an engineer. They need young guys like me. Yeah, Tommy swung that. He's doing pretty good.'

'And how's your job here?' There was an awkward silence.

'I don't think about that now,' he said. Say, why don't you come and have a beer with us, John? I've just finished my shift.'

I was standing on the edge of the top step, holding the door open. The freshness of the air swept my face. I rocked onto the balls of my feet, savouring the moment. Eldridge's face was bright and expectant. There was no reason why I should not spring down from the train and go off with him. Suddenly the carriage hissed beneath me, and there came a roar from the front of the train.

'Make up your mind, John,' said Eldridge. 'Train's gonna go.'

That was it, the great noise of the train had decided me. I jumped down to Eldridge's side, and together we walked across the tracks towards the steep bank. Behind us the train shuddered away into the city.

As we approached the house I heard a sinuous melody coming

down the street towards us; Tommy was playing at his open window. I slowed my steps, so that Eldridge got ahead of me, and listened intently. I had come to associate that sound with night, and in particular with that shameful night at the rent party. Now it was like dawn lighting a landscape I had not known to exist.

Eldridge looked back. 'C'mon, John. What you doing?'

We went into the house and up to Tommy's room. He was standing at the window with his eyes closed, playing the same fragment of melody over and over again.

'Say, Tommy,' said Eldridge. 'Look who's here. Our bum from the railroad.'

He looked round. 'John, where you been?'

'I had a job with Mr S—— . . .'

'He fire you?'

'No, I left.'

'That was a good move, 'cause there's plenty for you to do here. I got a job for you.'

'Let's go get a beer,' said Eldridge.

'Sure,' said Tommy. 'We got plenty to discuss.'

Lennox was bright and colourful. As we turned into it, two smart young African couples swept past us, the men in tight-cut suits and hats, the women in flowery dresses. There were women pushing prams, earnest young men hurrying along, children knocking balls about.

'They should keep these kids off the sidewalk,' said Eldridge as one of them ran under his feet.

Tommy was drinking in the scene. 'This,' he said, 'is the finest street in the city.'

We went into the bar where I had met Peewee. Jake was playing at the piano. His stamping chords were as unstoppable as a heavy barrel rolling down a mountainside.

'Hey, Jake,' cried Tommy, 'John's back.'

Jake stopped and looked round with a broad smile. We went and sat with him while Eldridge went to the bar for a pitcher of beer.

'You hear about Peewee?' Jake asked me.

'No.'

'He died. It happened the other night. He was sitting on his usual stool over there, and just keeled over and died. We reckoned the drink must have got to his heart. So it looks like you've got permanent possession of a fiddle.'

'Didn't he leave a will?'

'You kidding? He couldn't even write.'Sides, that fiddle was the only thing he had, and that's best off with you.'

'Well, I'm sorry he died.'

'That's good of you. He sure didn't have a lot of people to mourn him.'

Eldridge returned and poured our drinks.

'You tell John about this record contract?' Tommy asked him.

'Course I did.' He beamed round at us. 'You guys really hitting the big time.'

'How about you, Eldridge?' said Jake. 'You doing all right on the railroad?'

'No, I'm gonna turn it in. They passed over me for a promotion. Damned if I'm gonna spend the rest of my life digging holes.'

''Cause I was thinking,' Jake continued, 'if we're gonna start messing with the record companies, that'll get us a whole lot more dates. We're gonna need a manager to sort out the contracts and stuff and make sure we don't get screwed. Fix up dates and that kind of thing. You gotta do it proper. You think your brother'd fit the bill for that job, Tommy?'

'I don't know about that,' Eldridge interrupted. 'I got me an interview with the record company. You get into a big organisation like that and you can work your way right to the top.'

'You kidding yourself or what?' said Jake. 'You'd be in exactly the same position as you was on the railroad. They ain't interested in helping along a nigger like you. You come in with us and you'd be your own boss. Hell, you'd be *our* boss.' He laughed. 'You do the job proper, and you take a cut of the money we make. What do you say?'

Eldridge looked at his glass dubiously. Then he looked round at Tommy and me. 'What do you guys think?'

Tommy shrugged his shoulders.

'I really don't know about that,' said Eldridge. 'I'll have to think about it.'

We began discussing the future of the orchestra in earnest.
When we had eaten some lunch we strolled back to the house.

'Tell you another thing,' said Tommy as we climbed the stairs
to his room, 'we need a new bass. That guy we got at the moment
just can't cut it.'

'Guess you're right,' said Jake. 'I heard Johnny Williams looking
for some work at the moment. I'll give him a call.'

'Yeah, that guy's useful.'

Jake picked up the guitar, sat down beside Eldridge on Tommy's
pallet, and strummed some chords. 'We'd better check our fiddle
player still up to it. You want to do an audition, John?'

I picked up the bow and felt it balance between my fingers.
'Very much,' I said.

Jake played a short introduction. I picked up the violin and
began to play the blues. It was wonderful to perform once more;
one never knows what one has missed until it is found again. The
bow was like a rapier in my hand. I cut and thrust, then lashed
the strings as though they were but pieces of straw blown
this way and that in the wind. When I had finished Jake just
smiled.

'Get your horn out, Tommy,' he said. 'I've got a new tune for
you two.'

He played us a sequence of chords. Tommy began to improvise
softly above them.

'C'mon, John,' urged Jake, 'just jam on these chords.'

As I joined Tommy in feeling a way across the strange harmonies, it was as if we were traversing a landscape. I could see us
from far above. There were moments of intricacy and hesitation,
like the fording of a stream. Then there were passages when the
tension rose, as though we were climbing a hillside – only to be
released as we ran whooping down the other side. After several
cycles, Tommy left me and I continued alone – tentatively at first,
pulled on by the chords, then with greater boldness, until I was
anticipating and urging on the shifts in harmony. I tired, my
melody sank to the lowest string, and Jake began to sing.

I stopped and sat down beside Eldridge on the pallet. Jake had
scarcely sung a verse when the door opened and May came into
the room. Tommy had taken up his horn, and was playing in

harmony. She looked at me long and hard. The only thing that moved in the close, stuffy room was the song.

There was a long silence after the last chord had died away.

'He quit his job,' said Tommy breathlessly.

'So, you find out any about the CAU, then?' May asked me fiercely. 'You do any spying down there?'

'No,' I said, 'I'm afraid I didn't.'

'Shouldn't you still be down there then? I thought that's why you went?'

'Those were only my reasons initially,' I confessed. 'I then became ambitious, but with an ambition that was not my own. I was seized by a desire to be at the heart of affairs, and control them.'

'Why d'you quit then?' asked May. Her tone was less harsh.

'Because I realised I didn't belong there –'

'He's a musician!' protested Tommy.

'– and that there was no reason for me to stay. I do beg you to take me back.'

'I don't understand you, man,' said Eldridge. 'That was a good job you had there.'

That was all I felt able to tell them on the subject of my leaving Mr S——. But there was more than that going on in my mind. For ever since the previous morning, I had been thinking about why Mr S—— should bid in his own auction. The explanation had come to me, and brought me to recall an incident that occurred some four years ago, when I was physician on the slaver. I never told you about it when I wrote to you from the Indies, because I felt ashamed about the business. But I have resolved to be open in this, my last letter to you. And besides, I no longer feel ashamed about the matter.

The *Opportunity*, you may remember, Father, was the ship of Mr Harnham's that I was assigned to. The *Opportunity* had put in at a small port on the Gold Coast, and the captain had sent me ashore to conduct diplomacy with a local king. My instructions were to placate this man and do his bidding, with a view to securing the purchase of sixty slaves his men had captured inland and were bringing to the coast. There was a period of some two weeks before these slaves would arrive, and the king asked me in the meantime to act as one of his agents in the sale of a smaller number of slaves to local traders. Four local traders were engaged in bidding for these slaves, and the bidding was, by custom, done in private, with each contestant ignorant of the sums offered by the others. A closing day for the auction was fixed for ten days' time; whoever held the highest bid on that day would win the purchase.

I was assigned by the king to the wealthiest of these traders, to become his friend and confidant. Every evening for ten days I would go to this man's hut, drink his wine, eat his meat, and advise him in secret whispers – as I had been instructed – that if he would only raise his bid a fraction more then he would be ahead of his competitors. So his bid went up, and came the day of the auction's closing, my man won the purchase.

But rumours began to fly around the village. My man went around the other traders and discovered – to his fury, and my complete surprise – that the others' bids were much lower than the king had intimated to him through me. The king had coolly tricked him out of a large amount of gold and, what was worse, made him the butt of local ridicule – and I, I confess, had been the king's dupe in all of this. The fury of this trader was now directed at myself, who had abused his hospitality and robbed him of his gold and his standing. It was evidently useless to remonstrate with him that I had been as innocent as he; as soon as I heard that some hired ruffians were out to get me, I fled back to the ship without the slaves whose possession I had originally been sent to secure.

Now it was no concern of mine, Father, how Mr S—— conducted his own business. No, it was the simple fact of the association in my mind that made me think of fleeing him. But then Mr S—— had from the start been connected, for me, with the thought of flight. I had fled Tommy's family to be under him, and I had placed myself under him in order, in time, to flee from him. Now, it seemed, I faced a choice between a pursuance of this life of flight, and a quite different life in which there was no fear and flight. It was as though it were early morning, and there had suddenly sprung to mind the alternatives of dashing out into the day or of sitting down to write a letter.

Tommy viewed the matter in quite a different spirit. 'You want my advice,' he said, 'you'll stay out of politics.'

I stayed. For Tommy's family were good enough to take me back. Two evenings after my rearrival, May came to me as I was practising my violin in Tommy's room.

'I met another English guy at the office today,' she said. 'His ship's going back there in a couple of weeks. I mentioned you to him. He said he'd give you passage if you wanted. Well? You wanna take it?'

I cast a glance out of the window across the roof-tops.

'No. I'll stay.'

'Well, if it's all right here for you, then that's okay with me.' She smiled.

It was at that moment that I conceived the idea of writing to you. I asked May to inquire of the English trader whether he would take back with him a letter for my father, and the next day I began this account.

Every moment of our lives is a spoke in the rolling wheel of time. For you, I am gone. But I am elsewhere. The mind is fired by absence, by the non-existent strains of music that are neither in the vibrations of strings nor the movements of the air, but nowhere. When it struck me that I would never see you again, I was seized by the desire to reach you. I remember when I was a boy you went to great lengths to procure me a copy of Handel's sonatas. It could only be obtained, at great expense, in London. I pored over that score for months, and marked it carefully with fingerings and bowings. Yes, the further you go back, the heavier is the luggage of the past. That boy, ten years on, was to try to pack that luggage in a trunk and take it off to sea. As the poet says: 'The whistle of youth died on the ageless wind . . .' The luggage would not fit. Even now my mind seems lumpy. There are bulges. Especially back there, where the heaviest baggage is, at the bottom of the sack.

For two weeks I have written day and night. Tommy has grown impatient with me for missing rehearsals. We have a number of important concerts soon, and our first recording. And then we are going on tour; I shall see more of this strange land I have made my home. But first I had to fulfil this obligation I felt towards you. I am writing this now on a packing case at the dockside. I am due to meet our messenger soon. The ships, vast like whales beside the buildings, are idling in the waters. I like to think of them breaking out from the confines of the harbour into the open sea, and I like to think of the passage that this missive will take. But I feel no desire to follow it. You may remember how when I first met Eldridge he called this the 'land of freedom'. I think I recounted the scene with irony. I do feel something of the breath of freedom here, something that it is dangerous to put into words, that can only be put into music, or life. So, please do not worry that I have regrets. Think only with affection of your loving son,

John Field